Marrying the Admiral's Daughter

Lynda Dunwell

. . .

A Sweet Regency Romance

. . .

Romantic Reads Publishing

www.RomanticReadsPublishing.com

. . .

Marrying the Admiral's Daughter
First published by Musa Publishing in the USA
November, 2011 in ebook format

This edition by Romantic Reads Publishing
Staffordshire, United Kingdom
Copyright © 2015 Lynda Dunwell
All rights reserved.
ISBN:978-0-9574837-6-7
ISBN-13:9780957483767

To my family and friends

ACKNOWLEDGMENTS

Thanks to the dedicated team at Romantic Reads Publishing, especially editors Betty Turner, Maggie Glynn and fellow author and beta reader Heidi McAnna.

Cover Design:
Selfpubbookcovers.com/Lori

Other books by Lynda Dunwell

Regency Romances

Captain Westwood's Inheritance
Colonel Weston's Wedding

Historical Romances

Tomorrow Belongs to Us: Titanic Series

Titanic Twelve Tales:
Short Story Anthology

Historical Crime/Romance

Josh Walker Investigates Novels:

What is Love's Sign?
The Mayor's Mistress (2015)
Death of an Artist (2015)

Chapter One

June 1802

"Female demi-nudity!" Lady Mary leaned closer to her friend as they travelled home in the Richmond carriage. "*The Lady's Monthly Museum* says what for the Season?"

Bella pointed to the article in the magazine she had acquired during their Portsmouth shopping trip. "I quote 'the close, all white, shroud looking, ghostly chemise undress of the ladies, who seem to glide like spectres…now sheer undressing is the general rage.'"

"Now I comprehend why Madame Irene suggested the diaphanous white silk."

"When she opened the bolt and ran her hand under the fabric, it was nearly transparent." Bella dropped the printed sheets onto her lap. "London will always dance to fashion's drum. Why should I follow? Besides, I'm too old for white."

"At three and twenty?"

"Regardless of my age, I'm not prepared to go gliding around a ballroom *en chemise*."

"Not even at my summer ball?"

"Definitely not! Let girls in their first Season go half-naked to secure a husband. My blue silk will suit me fine."

"You don't make the most of yourself these—" Lady Mary gasped as a violent jolt unseated them. Wheels screeched. Horses snorted. The coachman bellowed at his team, and the carriage came to an abrupt halt.

"By all the saints!" Bella struggled to get back to her seat, shaken and her bonnet askew. "Mary, are you hurt?"

Kneeling, Lady Mary put her hands to her head and straightened her hat. "I'm unharmed. I've endured worse at sea. And you my dear, I hope the shock has not upset you."

Bella helped her friend to the seat beside her. "Be assured, although unseated, I am not distressed."

"Thank goodness, for I have no notion what I would have told your father." She turned to Bella's maid, a small middle-age woman sprawled on the opposite seat. "Are you injured, Miss Roberts?"

The woman rubbed her elbows. "Only a few bruises, my lady."

Satisfied they had suffered no serious harm, Bella tucked her blonde curls back under her bonnet and leaned out of the carriage window. "What's afoot Pride?"

"A fallen tree has blocked the road, Miss," the coachman replied.

"Can't you round it?"

"Ground's too uneven, Miss."

The young boy riding with the coachman ran past and grabbed hold of the lead horses. Before Bella could give further orders, the sound of pounding hooves approaching made her look back down the road. Four riders emerged from the trees and surrounded the carriage. A pistol shot rang out.

"We're under attack, take cover!" Bella shouted. The shot startled the horses and the carriage rocked.

She sank to the floor beside Lady Mary and the maidservant. "What do they want? We've no money."

"Highwaymen take anything of value. Where does your father keep the pistols?" Lady Mary asked.

Stunned, she glared at her mentor, then at Miss Roberts who cowered on the floor, her hands wrapped around her head. In desperation, Bella fumbled under the seat and pulled out a wooden box. The lid opened easily. "Damnation! It's empty."

"Have courage, both of you," said Lady Mary. "Keep quiet and only speak when they address you. I doubt these villains want our lives."

"I pray you are right." Bella grasped her older friend's hand as a mounted figure appeared at the window. He leaned forward and wrenched open the carriage door.

"Get out!"

Bella held her breath as she stared down the barrel of the highwayman's pistol. With a dark kerchief tied around his lower face and a battered tri-cornered hat pulled well down over his forehead, only his small, menacing eyes were visible. He slid down from his saddle but kept the pistol pointed at them. Standing with his feet apart, his square-shouldered frame swathed in a heavy boat cloak, he looked a formidable enemy.

Bella edged her way to the door, swung her legs down from the carriage, and pulled her muslin skirts around her. Spine-tingling fear crept down her back as she struggled to keep her lower lip from trembling. Gripping the sides of the carriage door, she placed her feet on the ground and slowly stepped away from the carriage. Afraid to make any rapid movement, she stood in silence as the highwayman took a pace towards her.

Inwardly she wanted to rail against this man who threatened her liberty, but self-preservation prevented her from crying out. She swallowed deeply when his eyes swept over her, as if he was assessing her worth.

A few moments later, Lady Mary climbed down and stood shoulder-to-shoulder beside her. The warmth of her body brought Bella some comfort, especially when the firm grip of her friend's hand interlocked with her own.

"Where is the other female?" The highwayman directed his pistol at the carriage door.

"My…maid?" Bella uttered.

"Only a servant," Lady Mary said. "Miss Roberts, come out!"

The highwayman threw the reins of his horse at one of the other masked men, pushed past the ladies, and jumped into the carriage. Within seconds he emerged with the maid screaming. Dragging her by the hair, he flung her to the ground.

Horrified by his treatment of her beloved servant, Bella rushed to her aid. The poor woman sat huddled on the ground shaking and sobbing.

"Leave her be!" The highwayman prodded Bella with the barrel of his pistol. It felt hard and cold against her shoulder. She took a deep breath and slowly rose to her feet. "Now you will do as I order." He turned the weapon in the direction of the box. "Driver, get down from there at once!" When Pride didn't move, the gang leader cocked his pistol and took aim. "Maybe you desire to meet your Maker?"

Aghast, Bella cried, "Pride, do as ordered." Relieved when the coachman began to move, she turned to Lady Mary, "I believe these brigands are French!"

"*Mais oui,* and proud sons of the Republic." He chuckled and pointed the pistol back at Bella. She was bewildered. What did Frenchmen want? They had not demanded money. And why had they treated a middle-aged servant with so much force? She felt her head begin to swim and the bitter taste of bile in her mouth. Trying to steady herself she stepped back but caught her heel in a rut in the road and fell over.

Lady Mary crouched beside her. "Are you hurt?"

"No, but what are we going to do?"

Lady Mary shrugged and placed a comforting arm around Bella's shoulders. In doing so she leaned closer and whispered. "We must keep our heads and refuse to be intimidated. Do not let them know we understand their language. I've been under French attack at sea. If they intended to kill us, we'd be dead by now."

"Driver!" the leader yelled. "Are you deaf? Secure the straps. Move!" He gave his men a string of orders in French. They unhitched the horses, dragged Pride along the ground and bound him to a nearby tree with his young assistant.

Meanwhile, Lady Mary helped Bella to her feet. "Should their intention be violation, I cannot stand by and let them ruin you."

Bella grasped her friend's arm. "Don't do anything foolish, Mary."

The gang leader sauntered towards them. "You, the young one, I'll get a good price for you."

"You will not!" Lady Mary drew a small pistol from her reticule and pointed it at him.

"Imbecile! Drop the weapon or my men will open fire!"

Bella's mouth fell open. She could not allow her dear friend to sacrifice herself. The odds were against her, four to one. If Mary wounded the leader, he might still fire his weapon. And at short range, it could mean certain death. "Do as he says, Mary, please!"

For a few moments, Lady Mary didn't move. Her face was locked in an expressionless glare. Bella's heart squeezed with tension as she willed her friend to lower her weapon. Slowly, Lady Mary let the pistol fall to the ground.

"We 'ave no time for foolish gestures." The leader of the gang grabbed Bella's arm. She screamed when he pulled at her bonnet, causing the velvet ribbons to bite into her neck. Her fingers flew to her throat to release the bow and her blonde curls tumbled onto her shoulders. "Ah! We have a lively one." He held the hat out in front of her. "Come on, come and get it."

She stood her ground, her eyes fixed on him as he threw the bonnet over his shoulder. "What do you want?"

He ignored her and wrapped his free arm around her slender waist. With one powerful jolt, he dragged her against him. With her back against him she kicked him with her heels. He howled and pushed her away. Cursing her in French, he took aim and discharged his pistol into the ground at her feet. "Next time I shall kill you!"

Bella froze. Nausea welled up inside her. His hand on her shoulder he pulled her around to face him. Belting the empty pistol, he used both his hands to tear open the front of her spencer and gown. She clenched her hands so tightly she could feel her nails digging into her palms. Determined not to show how humiliated she felt, she bit down on her lower lip. What did he expect of her? To beg for mercy? He grabbed hold of the torn front of her gown and dragged her towards him until she was within a few inches of his masked face. He smelled of horse, garlic and fish. She gasped when he seized hold of her blonde curls and jerked her head back.

"Leave her be! Take me instead!" Lady Mary cried.

"We want spring chickens, not old hens! Gag these women. Bind their hands and feet." He thrust Bella towards Lady Mary and repeated his orders in French.

The masked men worked quickly. From behind, one man encircled her arms, preventing her from struggling, while another bound her ankles together. She started to scream but a foul smelling gag was forced into her mouth and tied tightly behind her head. Only when her wrists were crossed and tied in front of her, did the first man let her go. She tried to hobble a few steps, anxious to see what they were doing to Lady Mary and Miss Roberts. But before she could look around a pair of rough hands seized her, swept her off her feet, and slung her over the back of a carriage horse. The men secured her wrists and ankles to the harness and draped a heavy boat cloak over her.

Bella's world went black as the smell of warm horseflesh pervaded her nostrils. She took short breaths and strained her ears, hoping to glean some clue of what was happening to the others. Some distance away, she heard the drum of riders followed by the crack of pistol fire.

She heard a voice shout, "*Allez!*" The carriage horse beneath her moved off. Where were they taking her? Tied over the horse's back, blood rushed to her head. All she could smell was horse sweat. She felt so helpless; the wrist and ankle bindings rubbed her flesh with every step the animal took. What did they want?

Restrained and powerless, her situation was desperate; nevertheless, she was determined to escape. But how? If she fell to the ground, it could easily be the end of her. Perhaps when they stopped and cut her free, she could get away. But how far could she run? Her abductors had pistols, horses, and far greater physical strength. Her situation felt hopeless, yet she clung to the belief that they would stop soon. At least then she might be freed from the discomfort of being slung over a horse's back. She heard the call to halt. As her horse slowed to walk, the sounds changed to the clomp of horseshoes on cobbles. When they did stop, the men spoke in raised voices.

"How much will we get for the blonde?"

"A good price but we must get back to harbour, the ship sails on the evening tide."

Bella calculated that they had four hours until high tide, plenty of time to reach Portsmouth on horseback. Why did they want her? Was she to be sold to some den of iniquity or the slave trade? What had happened to Lady Mary and Miss Roberts? Who were the riders she had heard when they left so abruptly? Would Pride, or someone else, come to her rescue?

In London she had heard tales of dark places where young women were held captive. But surely someone would help her. As a retired admiral, her father wasn't without influence. Silently she prayed for an end to her terrible situation.

The combined stench of straw and ammonia hit her nostrils. It made her stomach turn until she realised—they were in a stable. Perhaps they were going to rest here? Would there be a chance to escape? Her hopes lifted.

The men argued, speaking rapidly but too far away for Bella to understand everything they said. Only able to make out the odd phrase or two, she thought they intended to split up. But as the men came closer, she heard one man say, "The English, they are pigs. Who else would inhabit this God-forsaken land? We must run for the coast."

"Those men are not far behind. It will not take them long to find us."

"Do not panic, my friends." Instantly Bella recognized the voice of the leader. "We will trade the horses and leave the woman behind. We do not have time to take her with us. Besides, she will slow us. It is a pity, I know, but she hasn't seen our faces, so how can she identify us? Come on my friends, let us go, quickly."

Someone cut the rope tethering her to the harness but left her wrists and ankles bound. Strong hands grabbed her hips from behind and tied the boat cloak around her body keeping her head covered. Pulled from the horse's back, she struggled when her feet touched the ground. Pushed from behind she landed face down on something soft. The stench was vile.

Bella waited in the blackness and strained her ears for any sound. Slowly she breathed through the muslin gag. Taking in air through her mouth lessened the foul smell from the stable floor. She held each precious breath for as long as possible.

Footsteps approached. They sounded heavy, male with the clink of spurs. They came closer until their owner must have been standing over her. Had one of the highwaymen returned?

She kept very still as the rope around her middle went slack. Her heart pounded. Her temperature soared. Hands clenched together, she had no idea what she was going to do the moment the boat cloak was removed. Instinct prevailed and hands locked together, she lashed out like a wounded animal at the figure before her. He lurched back, out of her reach.

"I mean you no harm, ma'am. I'm not a robber, see I'm not masked." Smiling, he knelt on one knee and removed his hat. "Captain Ross Quentin at your service, ma'am. If you will allow me to release your bindings, I'm sure you will be more comfortable."

She nodded, but gasped when he drew a knife from the top of his boot.

"To cut through the rope." Gently he released the muslin gag from her mouth.

Relief flooded through Bella's veins as she gazed in the semi-darkness at her broad shouldered rescuer. Acute embarrassment followed when she looked down at her dishevelled appearance. Whatever must he think of her? Clothes torn and muddied, no bonnet and her hair loose around her shoulders. She pulled the ripped front of her velvet spencer together and smoothed her other hand over her muslin gown. "My name is Miss Bella Richmond. I would be grateful if you could help me quit this vile place. I was travelling with my friend…Oh! Goodness, they were abandoned off the Aston Road."

"Be assured, Miss Richmond, my manservant has set them free. Please allow me to escort you back to your carriage and your friend."

"But the highwaymen, they might return."

"I doubt it."

In the semi-darkness of the stable, her pent up fears drained away as she took the arm of the strikingly handsome officer. Although a stranger to her, she sensed she could trust him. "Captain Quentin, although we have not been formally introduced, I am grateful for your assistance."

"I only wish to be of service, Miss Richmond, and restore you to your rightful place."

The late afternoon sun stung Bella's eyes when she emerged from the stable. Reluctantly she let go of the captain's arm and rubbed her eyelids until she could accommodate the change in light. When she opened them, her eyes rested upon his face and she couldn't prize them away.

His features were well-formed, sporting thick dark eyebrows, a straight nose, and a dimpled, angular jaw. The cut of his coat was superior and his cravat was tied in a modest fashion. What struck her most was the strength in his face. Some might regard his complexion as weather-beaten, but to her, his ruggedness only added to his appeal. He had introduced himself as a captain, although he wore no uniform and she wondered if he was military or naval, like her father. "Lady Mary Rufford and I were travelling home when we were set upon by highwaymen."

"Did you say Rufford? Wife to Captain Rufford?"

"Yes, but regrettably she has been a widow these past six years. Are you acquainted?"

"I believe we were introduced some years ago in Madeira. I thought there was something familiar about the lady."

"I'm sure she will be only too happy to renew your acquaintance." Bella smiled at him, and felt a twinge of guilt that their eyes had been locked together far too long for such short an acquaintance.

"Your carriage is probably three or four miles away. Are you able to ride Miss Richmond?"

"Only side-saddle."

His forehead creased. "I would advise urgency and discretion. Perhaps you can sit behind me across my saddle? May I suggest you wrap the boat cloak around yourself? If we were seen together on the road, I might be taken for your abductor."

"Of course, Captain, but please excuse the state of my dress, not to mention my need for a bath."

"Fear not, Miss Richmond, there is nothing about your apparel to give cause for offence."

* * * *

When they arrived at the Richmond carriage, Captain Quentin dismounted and held out his arms for Bella to slip down from the tall hunter. Once again, she felt the comfort of his strong arms about her. But it was the overwhelming relief when Lady Mary appeared at the carriage window that claimed her immediate attention. She rushed towards her friend.

"Oh, my dear, I feared for your safety. Are you unharmed?" Lady Mary asked.

"All is well," Bella breathed, "apart from my apparel, which can soon be fixed."

"I was so worried, my dear, I had no notion of what I was to tell your father." Quentin's manservant stepped forward and opened the carriage door. Lady Mary got down and held her young friend at arms' length. Discreetly she examined the state of Bella's attire under the oversized boat cloak. "Nothing untoward happened at the hands of those brigands?" Bella shook her head. "Then let's hope no one notices your gown until you are more presentable."

"Forgive me, Mary…I acted foolishly."

"Nonsense, my dear, your behaviour leaves nothing to be desired. You were very brave, and your father should be very proud of you. If he is not, I shall jolly well tell him he ought to be."

"We owe our gratitude to Captain Quentin. He found me after I'd been abandoned. I understand you may have been acquainted some years ago. Do you remember him?" She turned towards the captain and smiled.

Lady Mary straightened herself to her full height. "Captain Quentin, I believe we were introduced in Madeira." She offered him her hand. "Thank you for your assistance."

Quentin took her hand and bowed. "Thank you for remembering me, Lady Mary. I only wish the circumstances of our re-acquaintance had been less dramatic."

"Indeed, Captain Quentin, however, let us not forget the formalities. May I present my friend, Miss Richmond, daughter of Admiral Richmond."

It seemed strange to Bella to be acknowledging the captain formally after she had ridden behind him with her hands clenched tightly around his waist. However, she made her brief curtsey to him.

"I am delighted to make your acquaintance, Miss Richmond. I hope this afternoon's events have not proven too taxing for you to continue your journey?"

"All I wish, Captain Quentin, is to return home as soon as possible," Bella said.

"And I trust none of your party has suffered serious injury?" Quentin looked from one lady to the other.

Lady Mary replied, "I'm pleased to report we're unharmed but for a few bruises, although Miss

Richmond's maidservant was badly treated by the leader of those ruffians and is resting in the carriage. We are all grateful that you and your man were in the vicinity. You took an enormous risk, Captain. You were outnumbered two to one."

"We made as much noise as possible and hoped they would take flight. As luck would have it, they did. Unfortunately we didn't have the manpower to bring them to book. Are highwaymen a problem hereabouts?"

While he spoke, Bella sensed an unfamiliar tension building inside her. As if time had slowed, she felt a warm, prickly sensation creep the length of her back bone. She dismissed it as delayed shock, but hoped she wasn't about to faint. She had never fainted in her life, and had no wish to begin now.

"I have never been accosted by ruffians on this road," Lady Mary said. "But it appears now we are at peace with France, England is crawling with miscreants. Do you know, I believe they were French!"

"They spoke French," Bella confirmed. As Quentin turned towards her, she caught his blue eyes glistening like flawless sapphires. She broke the eye contact, embarrassed by her dishevelled appearance.

A slight smile broke at the corners of his mouth. "Are we far from Aston Grange?"

"If you are looking for Sir Humphrey Westwood," Lady Mary answered, "it's unlikely you will find him there. He has not visited the Grange for years. Furthermore, I believe the house has been closed this past twelve months."

"My purpose is to view the estate with the prospect of taking the tenancy."

Lady Mary glanced at Bella. "Good news indeed. We might be neighbours. Will you ride with us? We will feel safer under your protection. I sent Pride to the inn for fresh horses. It shouldn't be long before he returns. If you could escort us back to Witton Abbey, I am sure Admiral Richmond will wish to thank you personally. Are you acquainted with him?"

Quentin shook his head. "Only by reputation, Lady Mary. To escort you will be a privilege and an honour."

"You are very kind, Captain Quentin," she smiled at him.

He acknowledged her with a brief nod then glanced along the road. "While we are waiting for Pride to return, Jackson and I will try to clear the fallen tree." He nodded a slight bow to both ladies before turning to collect his horse.

As he walked away, Bella sensed her pulse throbbing. She touched her face with the back of her fingers and confirmed the heat of reddening cheeks. If that wasn't enough, her stomach fluttered, as if filled with a colony of butterflies. What had come over her? It wasn't illness because she enjoyed robust health. Shock from the abduction? It would be easy to lay blame there, but she had to face the truth—Captain Quentin. How could one man, of whom she knew so little, have such an effect on her?

* * * *

On their arrival at Witton Abbey, Bella went immediately to her chamber. Lady Mary had assured her that she would take care of the introductions and explain to Admiral Richmond what had transpired. Within the hour, Bella joined them in the library. She wore a fresh muslin gown with her hair up in a simple style.

Admiral Richmond looked grave when she crossed the room. He opened his arms to her and dropped a brief kiss on her forehead. "Thank goodness you are unharmed, my dear."

She turned towards her rescuer, smiled, and felt a blush sweep over her. Quickly turning away, she hoped her pinked cheeks hadn't been noticed by the others and took a seat close to Lady Mary.

"Yes, I have heard the particulars," the admiral said. "You had a fortunate escape today although the entire situation gives me much concern." He looked at his daughter. "I trust your maid is recovering?"

"Yes, Papa, but I fear it will take time for her nerves to settle."

Admiral Richmond nodded his agreement. "Much obliged to you, Captain Quentin, it is most fortunate you happened to be in the locality. However, as a gentleman, I'm sure you understand how importune it would be to have the particulars circulated in the neighbourhood?"

"Certainly, sir."

Lady Mary added her agreement. "As Miss Richmond's friend and chaperone I would not wish any intelligence regarding any possible neglect of my duty towards her to be made general knowledge. I'm sure you understand, Captain?"

Quentin gave a curt nod. "Perfectly, Lady Mary."

Throughout the delicate conversation Bella had been observing Quentin. He was taller than her father, his dark hair cut short in the modern fashion and his thick eyebrows added strength to his face. However, it was the distinct dimple in his chin that intrigued her.

"We are agreed that all intelligence regarding this afternoon is kept in strict confidence," the admiral said.

Bella sat bolt upright. "Papa, surely all crimes should be reported to the local magistrate to ensure the offenders are apprehended."

Admiral Richmond approached his daughter who was seated in a comfortable armchair. He rested his hand on the wing of the chair. "If they can be caught."

"But these villains are roaming the countryside, terrorizing innocent travellers and abducting women to sell them into…goodness knows! It's our duty to stop them."

"Your sentiments do you credit daughter. However, without description and notion of their whereabouts, we are powerless."

Quentin stepped forward. "With respect, sir, from Miss Richmond's account, they are French. There cannot be many of Bonaparte's brigands roaming free around the English countryside."

"Precisely, Captain Quentin," agreed the admiral as he paced the library carpet. "Undoubtedly they ran for the coast anxious to catch the tide, otherwise why did they abandon Bella? Damage limitation is vital. Horses were stolen, but the real injury may be of a different kind. Those blackguards made off with my daughter. I will not have her reputation sullied."

"Your reputation is paramount, my dear Bella," insisted Lady Mary. "Sharp tongues could exaggerate the story. If your involvement with highwaymen and your discovery in a state of dishevelment became universally known, you would be ruined."

"I came to no harm." The words were out of her mouth before she knew it, but on reflection she did not want to make a public spectacle out of herself. People would talk behind her back, she would be pointed out at assemblies, girls would be cautioned not to allow themselves to fall into a similar predicament, and her name would be spoken with a hush. It could be a heavy price to pay for something that was not her fault.

"Take heed of Lady Mary's counsel." The admiral's tone was stern. "A lady's reputation is easily lost and almost impossible to regain."

"Yes, Papa."

The admiral turned to Quentin. "Do I have your assurance that today's events will not be broadcast?"

"Sir, you have my word as an officer."

The gentlemen shook hands.

"I will see to Pride and his assistant. Are you certain of your man?" the admiral asked.

"Indeed, sir."

Admiral Richmond turned to his daughter. "My dear, you must act with utmost discretion over the next few weeks. We do not know why you were abducted, but we can be sure those brigands had some plan afoot. They may return to the neighbourhood, therefore, you must not go out alone under any circumstances. And that, my dear, includes your early morning rides."

"But, Papa, I'm always accompanied by Pride or one of the grooms."

"Unfortunately, one man may be insufficient protection against four armed bandits."

Bella's heart sank. It had been a traumatic day, but the thought that she could no longer ride out each morning on her beloved mare, Merriweather, wounded her deeply.

Chapter Two

One week after the carriage incident, Bella sauntered into the hall from the garden. She removed her gloves and bonnet and handed them to Middleton, the butler, who passed them onto a waiting maid. Gazing at her reflection in the hall mirror, Bella thought about what poor substitutes her turn about the garden and visit to the stables were, compared to her morning rides.

Middleton turned the hour glass and sounded eight bells. The admiral liked the regularity of navy life and kept ship's time at Witton. Each morning, on hearing the signal, Admiral Richmond emerged from his chamber and descended the stairs. On this particular morning, he wore a black coat which made him look more like an ageing rector than a retired admiral.

"Any news about the Grange, Papa?" Bella hoped her question didn't sound too forward. The prospect of Captain Quentin becoming their near neighbour had occupied a considerable amount of her time during the past week. But she wasn't prepared to admit that to her father.

"As to Quentin taking the tenancy, I presume?"

Bella felt her cheeks pink. "I enquire strictly out of neighbourly interest."

"Of course, you do, my dear. I meant to tell you last night, but you had retired when I returned from Portsmouth. I saw the fellow yesterday." He sniffed the air. "Ah! Bacon." He turned on his heel and hurried into the breakfast room. Bella knew he would not talk until his belly was full. She followed him, helped herself to a moderate portion of bacon and coddled eggs, and joined him at the table.

Eating in silence gave her time to reflect on why a gentleman she had only met once, had such a remarkable affect upon her.

She wanted to know more about him, his family, his career in the service, and his plans for the future now that the country was at peace. But whenever she thought of him, she always pictured his bright blue eyes and raven-wing hair. She took a sharp intake of breath. How dreadful she must have looked in her muddy, torn gown. How much of her had he seen under the boat cloak? More importantly, what did he think of her?

She tried to push him to the back of her mind, but had little success. The uncomfortable feelings kept welling-up inside her, and she could not eat her breakfast. What was the matter with her?

Was he married? The stark revelation that he might have wife and family quashed her day-dreaming. She sat bolt upright and recalled the two proposals she had received during her one and only London Season.

The first suitor, a peer, flew into a rage when she refused him. He had constantly stared at her chest, which made her feel uncomfortable. His pompous conduct reminded her of Granville Richmond, her cousin, whom she had disliked since childhood. The second proposal came from an older gentleman, a widower with two young children. Although she had liked his company and mild manner, she had decided against the prospect of an instant family and rejected him. Thus, she had returned home unmarried but quite content.

The highway incident had changed her situation. Someone had tried to abduct her, possibly to sell her into slavery. More importantly, when she had least expected it, her head had been turned by a handsome face. She liked Captain Quentin and hoped they would be able to renew their acquaintance in the not too distant future.

"Papa, Aston Grange?"

"Quentin has leased the place with an option to purchase, given the right terms, of course. After he rescued you and Mary, I felt it my duty to enquire about the fellow. Wrote to a few acquaintances. Used my Admiralty connections. Consulted the Navy List. He has an excellent record by all accounts. Made Post Captain by the time he was twenty-five. Commands the *Diana*, a nice frigate."

"I've heard of her."

"I'd be astounded if you had not! You should be honoured to count her captain amongst your acquaintances. Back in April of ninety-eight, Quentin captured the hundred ton *Revanche* while patrolling off Madeira. Eighteen months ago he took the French Bordeaux raider *Scipion*. Take note, my dear, we have a hero in our midst. I saw him yesterday and promised I'd go and pay my respects today. I must commiserate with him over this infernal peace."

"But, father…isn't peace what we all want?"

Admiral Richmond gazed at his daughter. "Arabella, I thought you understood *some* political matters."

Initially, she felt his chastisement keenly. He only used her full given name when he was annoyed with her. But hearing they had a new neighbour raised her spirits. And furthermore, to learn Captain Quentin had enjoyed a highly successful naval career added to her joy. Her father's brief scolding was short-lived.

"You have a good brain. If only you had been born a boy, what an officer you might have made, but to welcome peace? I despair, Bella. Despair."

She resented her father's comment, but hoped it didn't show on her face. As an only child, she had imagined herself following in her father's footsteps. Once, while on board his ship in port, she had asked her mother, "When can I join Papa's navy?"

Her mother had smiled and replied, "Young ladies cannot join the navy."

"There are ladies on board the ships," she had remembered, protesting with the innocence of an eight-year-old. "I know because I've seen them."

"Perhaps, child, but they are wives of officers or seamen and sail under their husbands' authority."

"Can't we sail with Papa?"

"No, child, your father believes conditions on board a ship are too harsh for us. Our duty lies at home."

Years later, Bella had realized the true significance of her mother's words. Near to death, her mother had confessed, "I loved your father but I've felt so alone. Marry a naval officer and the sea will always be his mistress."

Although the admiral had retired, he kept a small sloop at Portsmouth. He sailed along the south coast when weather permitted as he preferred a sea passage to travelling overland by coach. Bella often accompanied him and loved sailing. "The *Vesta's* no longer under naval command." He often remarked. "Private ships can do as they please."

Ensuring her father had cleared his plate, Bella asked, "Now we're at peace can we visit France?"

"Are you determined to upset my constitution for the rest of the day?" The admiral's high forehead creased. "To set foot on that Republican land would be utter madness. General Bonaparte is a cunning fox. He has declared himself Consulate. He supports scientific research and sets up schools. And, yes, his people love him for it! However, the French are our enemies. Mark my words. They mean to re-equip their fleet and invade us!"

"Does the government think so?"

"Who knows what those nincompoops think, if they ever do! Our ministers make peace and preserve their positions, which they never ought to have filled in the first place. This peace is wrong. Bonaparte is a conqueror. He will only be stopped by someone stronger."

* * * *

From the moment Quentin signed the tenancy agreement for Aston Grange, he was determined to have the place ship-shape. The house had been closed for over a year, and there were no resident staff. He found some of the *Diana's* old crew languishing in Portsmouth and offered them work. They scrubbed the wooden floors, polished the oak panelling, and buffed up the brass work. Furnishings were cleaned, chandeliers washed, chimneys swept, cellars inspected, attics cleared, and the house provisioned as if it were a frigate being made ready for a long voyage. When they had finished, Quentin stood in the entrance hall of his new home. His heart swelled with pride at the remarkable transformation his men had achieved in a week.

One of the first visitors was the local cleric, Mr. Winters. A small man, dressed in black, he fitted his calling. He introduced himself and cordially invited the captain and his staff to the next Sunday service.

"I shall be delighted to attend, sir. At what hour?"

"We sound the bell towards eleven, sir, but do not worry if you are a little late. I shall not begin the service without you."

Quentin raised his eyebrows at Mr. Winters's remark, "Somewhat unusual, isn't that?"

"Goodness, no, Captain. I always waited for Sir Humphrey. Are you closely acquainted with him?"

Quentin shook his head. "We corresponded via agents. I hope to make his acquaintance when I'm next in town."

"I have always found him most obliging." He rubbed his hands together as he spoke. "When you do meet Sir Humphrey, would you be so kind as to convey my regards to him, Captain?"

"Of course, but I have no idea when I shall be going to town."

Mr. Winters nodded, then glancing about the drawing room said: "Sir Humphrey is fortunate in his choice of tenant, especially one as well-known as you, sir."

"You flatter me, Mr. Winters."

"No, sir, simply giving credit where it is due. There are many in the parish with sea-faring connections. Your reputation precedes you." He looked around again. "My congratulations, you have transformed this room. Unfortunately, the Grange has had many tenants.

Few have remained long. My wife tells me that the ladies complain about the draughts, especially at night."

"My staff and I neither feel the cold, nor do draughts disturb our slumber. The roof is sound. The rooms are dry, including the cellars. What more could a sailor want?"

The door opened and Jackson announced, "Admiral Richmond."

Mr. Winters sprang to his feet. "I'm sure as naval gentlemen you have much to discuss. I must be about my parish business." He acknowledged the admiral and took his leave.

* * * *

Later that day, Bella received Mrs. Winters. The parson's wife was a regular caller at Witton; she often visited the members of the parish and was a good source of gossip. Following the butler's announcement, she scurried into the small parlour. "I have glorious news which cannot be kept a moment longer."

Bella put down the book she had been reading. "Would you like some tea?"

Mrs. Winters nodded, her face filled with excitement. It was obvious that Mrs. Winters could contain herself no longer, so as soon as Middleton had quit the room Bella inquired as to the purpose of her visit. "Oh, joy! I have such wonderful news for the neighbourhood. I came the moment I had it from Mr. Winters direct. There's a new tenant at the Grange. Captain Quentin is a naval officer. He commands a frigate."

Bella had been instructed by her father to remain silent about her first meeting with Captain Quentin.

Therefore, she thought it wise to pretend to Mrs. Winters that she knew nothing of the gentleman. "How interesting. And is he of good family?"

"At present, I know little of his origins. Mr. Winters gave no details when he returned from the Grange. However, as Admiral Richmond also called at the Grange this morning, I assume Captain Quentin's credentials are satisfactory. Did your father not mention his visit?"

Bella thought for a few moments. Generally Mrs. Winters displayed good humour in her conversation, and although she had some of the reserve expected in a parson's wife, she was inclined to embroider her facts. However, her sources of basic intelligence were usually accurate. "Papa did imply that the Grange had a new tenant. Now tell me, is Captain Quentin a rising star?"

"A star?" Mrs. Winters looked puzzled. "I do not recall Mr. Winters describing him so."

Bella checked herself. She had to be careful what she said because Mrs. Winters would undoubtedly quote her elsewhere. "Frigate captains are the elite of the navy's commanders. They are paid less than ship-of-the-line captains, but that does not matter to them. Often they are lone hunters. The Admiralty can send them on independent cruises or employ them in operations outside of the orders of the station's commander-in-chief. They take prizes, make fortunes, and sail home with honour and glory."

"Oh, my goodness! Is the new tenant one of this breed of men?"

"Possibly so. Now, what else do you know?"

Mrs. Winters grinned. "The most important news and the very best - Captain Quentin is eligible."

Chapter Three

For the first time in years, a woman disturbed Ross Quentin's slumber. Alone in his bed, he wrestled with silky blonde curls cascading over cream shoulders. He closed his eyes and bathed in the alluring gaze of her brown eyes. He wanted to wrap his arms around her and feel the touch of her firm body against his, as he had done when she had sat behind his saddle.

He knew he had been lucky to find her that day. The stolen carriage horses had left droppings where they had been tethered outside the derelict stable. Prepared for the worst, he had ventured inside and discovered her. Nothing had prepared him for the way her presence had stayed with him during the following week.

He was accustomed to life at sea, but his situation had changed with the Peace of Amiens and he was thrust into a new life in the English countryside. Now he faced many new challenges. At sea, he was in command. On land, he had to conform to the rules of society.

Aware of his obligation to return calls made to him at the Grange, he made a visit to Witton. Wearing his new dark tail-coat, light buckskins, and highly polished black top-boots, he felt well turned out. So with a confident air, he strode into the library as Middleton announced him.

Admiral Richmond abandoned his newspaper, stood up and offered Ross his hand. "Your visit is most welcome, Quentin."

Miss Richmond greeted him formally with a slight bob. "Good afternoon, Captain Quentin."

"Miss Richmond." He allowed his eyes to range over her as she resumed her seat. Unaccustomed to polite conversation in the middle of the afternoon, he was grateful when the admiral offered him a seat, not too close to Miss Richmond but strategically positioned to secure a good view of her.

"I hear you have been very busy at the Grange attending to domestic arrangements."

"Indeed, Miss Richmond, my men are used to life at sea, they need occupation. I, too, am used to a certain degree of order. It has been a challenge to get the Grange ship-shape, but a very worthwhile one." He felt a degree of nervousness talking to her. It had been different when he had rescued her, or later that day when he had escorted her home to her father. Now, he was required to make conversation about nothing. What did a gentleman talk about to a young lady? He thought for a few moments. "Do you play and sing, Miss Richmond?"

"A little, although Papa prefers a game of chess to music."

"Never had the ear for a note." The admiral chuckled. "No rhythm either. Dreadful when I had to stand up in a ballroom. Now chess, there's a game. You have to work out your strategy. Plan your tactics. Trouble is Bella always beats me!"

"Would you like a game, sir?"

The admiral shook his head. "Nay, lad, but I'd like to see you play against Bella."

Engaging in a game of chess with the lady who disturbed his sleep, did not strike Ross as a good idea. It might provide an opportunity to become better acquainted with her, but would her proximity affect his ability to concentrate?

"Papa, we can't possibly impose on Captain Quentin's good nature. He came to pay his respects, not to be pressed into a chess contest."

"Please play, Bella. Come, Quentin, take a seat at the card table. Fetch the pieces, daughter." He rubbed his hands together. "I'm going to enjoy this."

Ross's gaze followed her as she rose and crossed the room. He could not stop himself admiring her neat figure. He liked the pale green shade of her gown, and the way her honey blonde hair was dressed in the Grecian style. Her features were small, especially her pert nose, but he particularly admired her dark brown eyes. He decided she was handsome without being pretty and that pleased him greatly. Silently, he amused himself with the possibility that Bella Richmond was not aware of her attractiveness. Surprisingly, he found the notion exceedingly engaging.

During his naval career, he had learned to be cautious of beautiful women. He had known several, usually the wives of his fellow officers. He had also experienced some of them flirting with the unattached young men. Drawn into a compromising situation, a young officer had little resistance against an experienced woman's advances, especially if she was a renowned beauty.

Miss Richmond returned, clutching a box. She set out the pieces on the chessboard and invited him to sit down. Only after she had taken her seat did he occupy the place offered.

She picked up a white pawn and made her opening gambit. "I hope you are not going to glare at me all through the game."

"Please forgive me, Miss Richmond." He looked at the chessboard and made his first move. As she had begun defensively, he decided to do likewise to gauge her measure. However, while she took her turns, he could not resist the luxury of watching both the chessboard and her.

The admiral, his arms behind his back, paced up and down, watching the run of play. "This isn't your usual game, Bella. Are your thoughts elsewhere?"

"No, Papa." She moved her knight into a defensive position, raised her eyes from the board, and turned them on her opponent.

Ross felt their full force, as she stripped bare his soul and siren-like, lured him towards dangerous waters. Somehow he had his fingers around his queen. He moved the piece the full length of the board and left a knight unsupported. Immediately, he saw his error. Too late. He watched her eagle eyes review any potential moves he might have had in reserve. Did she believe he had sacrificed himself intentionally? He nearly spoke, but thought better of it. Did she think he was testing her or patronizing her? Moving his queen had cut across his measured run of play. In silence, he waited for her reaction.

Miss Richmond took the knight and checkmated his king in four moves.

"I say, what a splendid victory." The admiral clapped his hands. "Makes me feel a hundred times better knowing I'm not the only one Bella beats. The Admiralty had better not give my daughter a ship-of-the-line. She would blast us all out of the water."

Ross smiled politely at the admiral's joke. Inwardly, he cursed himself for being diverted. Apart from losing the match, which annoyed him excessively, he had enjoyed every minute of it.

Miss Richmond started to collect the chessmen and place them in their box, avoiding his eyes. When she rose, he sprang to his feet. Ross felt disappointed the game appeared over. He intercepted her before she had the chance to cross the room. "Miss Richmond, surely you cannot leave me defeated with no opportunity for recovery?"

"That was not my intention, but please excuse me…I…must speak to cook." Her face began to pink.

"At least grant me the satisfaction of a re-match?"

She hesitated, as if to choose her words carefully. "Forgive me, Captain Quentin, if I do not rise to your challenge, but I must instruct the staff."

"Please don't leave." He glanced over his shoulder, ensuring they were out of the admiral's earshot before he continued, "It's an excuse, isn't it? What are you afraid of? Me or the revenge I might extort on the chessboard?" He knew he had touched a sensitive nerve as her pink cheeks grew even redder.

She looked straight into his eyes. "One game, Captain Quentin, and this time play to win."

Ross sensed a muscle-twitch in his lower jaw and struggled to control it. He nodded in agreement and looked away for a few seconds. Out of the corner of his eye he glimpsed the admiral smiling, obviously thoroughly enjoying the spectacle.

They returned to the table, and the rematch began. Again the game started with defensive moves. Outwardly Miss Richmond appeared calm, but that did not mean her feelings were unaffected. She was a gentleman's daughter, schooled in appropriate behaviour. He did not expect any display of emotion from her. Of course, that did not mean her feelings were untouched by the game. On the contrary, he hoped he was causing as much havoc to her sensibilities as she was to his.

Now he regarded her as a serious opponent. He had lost their first game due to his own diversion. He would never have done so at sea. Given a second chance, he could not afford to falter. The game progressed, veering this way and that. Eventually, when the tide turned, it was not in his favour.

The admiral hovered at the edge of the table. "I fear you're in an awkward position, Quentin, under heavy attack with little defence."

As he scrutinized the board, Ross could see his position was hopeless. Miss Richmond seemed capable of reading his every move. He looked directly into her velvet brown eyes and rather than hear her clear declaration of *"Check Mate"* twice in one day, he placed his hand on his king and brought him down.

"Forced to haul down your colours, eh?" The admiral chuckled. "Must be a first, Bella. I doubt if Bonaparte himself and the entire French fleet could get this man to surrender without a fight."

"Papa, this is but a game of chess, not a full scale naval engagement."

"Only a game of chess, eh? Oh, my dear, it was considerably more than that. Now Quentin, do feel free to call again whenever you wish. You will always be most welcome." He placed his hand on the captain's shoulder and looking at his daughter added, "I'm sure Bella will be more than happy to entertain you."

* * * *

As Mr. Winters's sermon droned on, Ross took out his gold pocket watch and checked the hour. Temptation crept up on him to release the chime. Perhaps the parson would take the hint and finish? From the pew allocated to Aston Grange, he had a restricted view of the rest of the congregation. He yearned for the freedom of his quarterdeck. From there, he could have taken his glass and set it wherever he wished, but not here. His mind wandered to the many things he would rather do than listen to the preacher for an hour.

Mr. Winters prattled on to the Aston parishioners. "There can be no finer way of demonstrating faith in the Almighty, than attending church on Sundays and listening, *in silence,* to the word of the Lord." Eventually, he made an end of it and the Aston parishioners made their way out of the church.

As soon as the Richmonds had acknowledged the parson at the church door, they approached Ross. "Good day to you, Quentin," the admiral said.

"And you, sir." Ross tipped his hat and smiled. "Good morning, Miss Richmond." He paused for a few moments to admire her appearance. Whenever he saw her, his heart gladdened. "Winters's sermons, are they always so drawn out? I saw some of my men had fallen asleep, and would have taken them to task, if we'd been at sea."

The admiral nodded. "I understand you perfectly. The parson is far too verbose, and his sermons are garbled."

Miss Richmond looked surprised by her father's gruff remark. "Despite its length, didn't you find the sermon engaging, Captain Quentin?"

"I did not." He hadn't expected his honest reply to bring the full force of her large brown eyes glaring at him, and he felt moved to offer an explanation. "Mr. Winters takes advantage of his parishioners."

"Indeed he does, Quentin," the admiral frowned, "and at your first service. The man has no consideration for his flock."

"Papa, I believe you are a little harsh on Mr. Winters. He attends to all his parish business himself, whereas there are other clergy who leave much to their curate."

"True," nodded the admiral, "but I fear it is his sense of his own importance that drives Mr. Winters. Is that not evident from the length of his sermons?"

Ross noted the brief nod between daughter and father, although he remained convinced Miss Richmond was not in total agreement with the admiral. He watched her glance over her shoulder, as if looking for a possible escape.

She turned back to face them. "Lady Mary is at the church door and she will want to greet you. I'll fetch her. Excuse me, Papa, Captain Quentin."

When his daughter was out of earshot, the admiral turned to Ross. "This sermon business, you can put us out of our misery. Instruct the man accordingly."

Ross shrugged his broad shoulders. "I do not understand, sir, how can I legitimately give orders to a man of the cloth in his own church?"

"Nothing to it, my boy. You are the tenant of Aston Grange. The parson's living and the fine house, of which he is so proud, is in the gift of the Grange, isn't it?"

"Aye, sir, but can a lease give me authority over the man?"

The admiral drew Ross to one side. "Mark my words. You may not be prepared to exercise your authority, but Winters does not know that. He tested the water this morning. Next week he will be up to an hour and a half, if you don't step in and clip his wings. It won't cause any harm and we can return to our homes while we can still feel our legs beneath us."

"Indeed?"

"Aye, swift action is the essence." He signalled the captain to come closer, "A quiet word will bring him to heel. Tell him twenty minutes and if he takes longer than half an hour, he can pack his bags. Once said, I'll wager the sermon's only a quarter of an hour by next week!"

****

Three estates made up the parish of Aston: Witton Abbey, Aston Grange, and Penley Court, the home of Lady Mary Rufford.

An earl's daughter, Lady Mary had eloped to Gretna Green when her father had refused permission for her to marry Charles Rufford. For fifteen years she had sailed with her husband, until he had succumbed to malaria in the West Indies. The Penley estate belonged to her brother, who had succeeded to the title.

"How delightful you look this morning." Lady Mary's eyes swept over the new gown and velvet spencer Bella wore. "I do like cream with burgundy and your bonnet is very fetching."

"I had a delivery from Madame Irene two days ago. The seamstress is a wonder. The three gowns she has made are lovely."

"I am pleased our shopping expedition to Portsmouth turned out favourable after all." She screwed up her eyes and squinted at Bella. "My dear, your complexion looks remarkably fine. I would say you are veritably blooming."

"The mild weather and regular exercise must be suiting my constitution," Bella said as they walked together.

They were soon joined by the admiral and Quentin who fell into step together, as did the ladies. The gentlemen led the way across the churchyard towards the lych-gate. Lady Mary took Bella's arm and the ladies followed at a slower pace.

"I do not want to be overheard," Lady Mary said, "but I understand the neighbourhood is quite taken with the captain. I am not surprised as he is held in high regard by his naval contemporaries. I expected him to be dashing but not so handsome. He was a tall, lanky fellow when I first made his acquaintance years ago. Now, I can see he has much improved."

"And I thought there was no other man for you but your beloved Charles."

"True, but neither marriage, nor widowhood, stops a keen eye admiring an attractive male of our species."

"Indeed?" Bella raised her eyebrows at her companion's frankness.

"Now, if I were but ten years younger, I might easily be persuaded to throw my hat into the ring. Although, I seriously doubt if I would stand a chance with my weathered complexion!"

"Nonsense." Bella loved the vigour of her friend but had to concede that her agreeable face was prematurely aged, undoubtedly the consequence of her married life at sea. However, her manner was open, her judgment honest, and her advice sound.

"I know my limitations. Besides, half of England will be clamouring at Captain Quentin's door, if they haven't already done so."

"Clamouring? Mary, whatever do you mean?"

"It's a universal truth. He has a fortune in prize money, and he is home for what must be the first time in ten years."

"Along with the rest of the fleet."

"Yes, my dear, but Quentin is part of our society, and the neighbourhood has decreed that he must need a wife!"

* * * *

"Jeremy, you weren't expected until tomorrow." Ross bellowed from the top landing above the hall. He descended the stairs two at a time and with a broad grin on his face shook his friend's hand. "Dashed glad to see you today."

"I had to get out of London. Elizabeth's in town with her sisters. Another one came out this Season. So, to escape warehouses of muslin and silk, I've come early. I hope that won't cause you any trouble."

"Trouble? When one of my oldest friends and comrades in arms arrives on my doorstep he is always welcome. Besides, look around you. Mr. Sanders has joined me as butler and what would I do without my old kellick, Jackson?"

Both men, former crew members on the *Diana,* stepped forward and welcomed the lieutenant. Ross ordered refreshments to be brought to the drawing room.

"So now you're back on land, how goes the wedding plans? Have you set the date?"

"Not I, dear friend. In the marriage game, your betrothed names the day, once the lawyers reach a settlement." He walked with Ross into the drawing room, followed by Jackson, who carried two tankards of ale.

"If not when, any notion of where?" Ross handed one tankard to his friend and kept the other himself.

Jeremy took a hearty swig of the brew and licked his lips. "Elizabeth's mother wants the wedding to take place in London. She hopes to snare another son-in-law this Season." Jeremy suddenly looked up from his mug. "Say, you wouldn't be interested, would you? I'm sure I could persuade her family of your kindly nature, friendly disposition, and large fortune. You would make the perfect bridegroom!"

"Your journey overland has addled your brain, Lieutenant Thwaite."

Jeremy smiled. "Just plain Thwaite will suffice now and Jeremy to you, dear friend."

Ross raised his tankard, "To friendship!"

"To friendship!"

When they had finished the ale, Ross offered to show his friend around the property.

"It's a grand house." Jeremy's eyes swept over the barrelled ceiling of the great hall. "Reminds me of the *Diana* with her panelling and oak decks. I suppose she'll be as draughty as the old lady in winter."

"Cynical as ever." Ross sighed. "The *Diana's* a good ship. She served us well and might do so again. I warrant the fleet might be back at sea soon."

"Have you heard something?"

Ross shook his head. "I spent my first week ashore camped outside the Admiralty until I was told, in no uncertain terms, that my war-mongering was derisive. Furthermore, if I valued my present position and wished to continue in His Majesty's service, I must remove myself forthwith."

"Ah! So what did you do?"

"Went to my club and got drunk."

"And did it help?"

Ross chuckled. "Gave me a thumping head for a day or so. Afterwards, I did the rounds of land agents and found this place. I wanted an option to buy, but the advice was to lease for the year."

"Wise decision. Get to know the lay of the land before you commit. What's the local society like? Have you set every female heart aflutter?"

"Not again. Be satisfied you are engaged. There's no need to infect everyone around you with the same rush of Cupid's arrow."

Jeremy shrugged his square shoulders. "Haven't you found a girl that interests you yet?"

Ross avoided the question. He did not want to admit that one young lady had taken his eye until he felt more certain of his own feelings. His acquaintance with Miss Richmond was short and he had heard that a man's fancy could be turned one week only to dissipate the next. Although he prided himself on his constant disposition, he had limited experience in matters of the heart. He decided he needed more time before he pursued his suit.

"Is anyone holding a ball in the neighbourhood? A dashing sea captain like you must surely be the guest of honour."

"Cut the flattery."

"Look at the advantage, my friend. A room full of hopeful young ladies, supported by their mothers and vying for your attention. As the toast of local society you could take your pick. If nothing took your fancy, you could dash up to town before the end of the Season. What better arrangement could there be?"

Ross thought for a few moments. Should he rise to his friend's goading? He leaned against the long oak table that stretched along one end of the great hall, his arms folded. "So, you would have me strut like a peacock at a ball?"

Jeremy shrugged. "Merely a suggestion."

"I suppose as tenant of a local estate I have some social responsibility to the neighbourhood, but I feel ill equipped to enter society. I've received one dance and supper invitation from Penley Court, which I intend to accept. As to a London Season? Most definitely not!"

Jeremy's face sank. "But you will come up to town, won't you, Ross? I'd rather like you to stand up for me as groomsman."

"Fear not, dear friend, rounding the Horn couldn't prevent me from attending your nuptials. I'd be honoured to stand as groomsman." He walked towards Jeremy, offered him his right hand, and slapped him on the shoulder with his left.

＊ ＊ ＊ ＊

Forbidden to ride, Bella took the carriage to Penley to call upon Lady Mary. As she alighted she saw her friend waving at her from the parlour window.

The butler led her directly to Lady Mary, who greeted her warmly. "My dear, you look very fetching.

Navy and cream are good colours for your complexion. Come, sit down by the window and tell me your news."

"Alas, if you crave news this morning, you will be sadly disappointed by my intelligence. I have very little which is new."

Lady Mary ordered hot chocolate for both of them. "Then be the first to hear mine. Another officer has arrived at the Grange, Lieutenant Thwaite. He was second in command to Captain Quentin on the *Diana*. But unlike our dashing hero, he has resigned his commission and is to be married to Lady Elizabeth Glen. According to my sister-in-law, rumour has it in town, that the marriage has only been sanctioned by the lady's family since the bridegroom became his father's heir. For his sake, I hope there is some mutual affection between the couple. I am told he is most amiable, but she is much under the influence of her mother. Let us hope it is a love-match. Now what is your position? Should marriage be for the heart or the head?"

"Oh, why must you persist with that old chestnut?" As soon as her words were spoken Bella regretted them. Her tone had been too severe. Softening her voice, she tried to explain. "I dislike talking about matters of which I have little personal knowledge."

"I thought you might have had a change of heart recently."

"Meaning?"

"According to my London correspondent, marriage is the most popular topic in town at present, so why shouldn't it be popular in the country?"

"Blame the Season and a wave of navy officers turned on shore since the peace."

"Possibly, but heart or head, what's your position?"

"Oh, Mary, if you insist on pressing me. Marriage is a permanent situation not to be entered into lightly. Although a love-match would seem the most exciting prospect, one must be practical. I imagine life without sufficient funds can be hard."

Lady Mary nodded. "Very wise, my dear, very sensible. Now, what do you want for yourself?"

Bella suspected a motive behind her friend's question. "I couldn't consider marrying a man for whom I had little or no affection. Thus, to marry solely for financial security would not suit me, if I had free choice. But I can understand circumstances when a woman may have no alternative. As for myself, I have no inclination to believe I might need matrimony. However, if I did, I would hope to find both."

"Fortunately, you weren't obliged to accept one of your offers during your Season. The gentlemen had funds and both failed to engage your heart. So, tell me, what manner of man must we seek to win over Miss Richmond?"

"So, you are scheming!" Bella took a few sips of her hot chocolate and tried to make light of the question. She knew she found the captain attractive but she wasn't prepared to admit the extent of her feelings, even to her best friend and confidante. "Don't you believe me when I say I've no intention of marrying?"

"But—"

"No buts." Bella held up her hand. "Why should I marry? I have the management of my father's establishment, and his assurance that a trust will be left for me. Currently I'm at liberty to exercise my own will without reference to a husband. I must accept my father's orders, but rarely does he prevent me from doing as I please, except riding at present. My position on matrimony hasn't changed since I came out. I have good reason to remain single, haven't I?"

Lady Mary looked thoughtful. "Put so, your argument is a convincing one, but what of the future? When the admiral is no longer with us, won't you be lonely?"

"Are you?"

"I have fifteen years of wedded bliss to console me. I have loved and been loved. My only disappointment was the marriage failed to produce issue."

The honest revelation surprised Bella. She had never heard Mary speak before concerning her lack of offspring. Mary had probably just exposed a small crack in her shell as a warning, but Bella didn't feel she had the right to pry any deeper. "I had no idea."

"Of course you didn't. Those matters are between husband and wife and should remain so. We were not blessed, and there's an end to it. However, it was not for the lack of trying." She smiled sheepishly.

Bella admired her friend's pragmatic approach to her barren state. It reflected her strong character and ability to cope with many of life's difficulties. "Oh, Mary, to view your situation with humour—you're very brave."

"Bravery has nothing to do with it. Charles was a splendid husband. Never did he blame me, or call me barren, not even in anger. Now I am reconciled with my family, and the role of a favourite aunt is my consolation. But I wonder, what will be yours?"

Chapter Four

When Bella arrived back at the Abbey, the butler told her that her father was entertaining Captain Quentin and Mr. Thwaite. "The admiral would be obliged if you would join them in the library, Miss."

Her heart skipped a beat, not only would she have the pleasure of the captain's company, but also, she could see how he conducted himself in the company of his friend. "Thank you, Middleton." She crossed the hall and hurried upstairs, calling for her maid along the way. A few minutes later she emerged wearing a fresh gown of muslin blue spot. She smoothed her hands over her face and bit her lips to make them look pinker. Taking a last look at herself in the hall mirror, she breathed in deeply and entered the library.

The gentlemen were deep in discussion around one of the library tables about a naval engagement. The admiral had a large chart spread out before them. Scattered over the chart was a set of wooden wedges he used to represent vessels when he demonstrated action at sea. "The Spanish fleet hauled wind on the larboard tack and made sail following a spirited attack by Nelson and Troubridge." The admiral looked up when she approached.

"Cape St. Vincent?"

"Aye, child. You see before you an old sea dog gleaning a few particulars from two officers who fought in the battle. It appears some of the accounts may have been inaccurate. Don't you remember, I said *The Times* correspondent appeared confused in his reporting?"

"Yes, Papa." Bella was only half-looking at her father when she replied; her actual attention was on Quentin. Her heart skipped, her stomach flipped over, and her neck flushed pink. She prayed the gentlemen didn't notice.

"We're busy putting the action to right. Forgive me, child. Let me introduce Lieutenant Thwaite, who served under Quentin."

Bella curtsied to both gentlemen, who bowed in response. "I trust my father hasn't neglected to offer refreshment?"

"Bah, tea!" grunted the admiral. "Ever the measure of a landlubber, always serving tea. Now aboard, we'd have—"

"But, Papa, it's only four o'clock." Bella protested, thinking of her father's gout.

"Gentlemen, it appears I have been remiss in my hospitality. I would offer you grog, but now that the lady of the house is with us, I suspect she will wish to serve us *dishes* of tea."

Acutely aware of the captain's eyes lingering perhaps a little too long on her, she took a deep breath. "Tea, gentlemen?"

Quentin smiled. "Tea would be most refreshing." He broke eye contact with her and looked at his friend, who nodded his agreement.

"If you'll excuse me for a moment, I'll make the arrangements." Stepping out of the library, she sent a footman to the kitchen with instructions for tea. When she returned to the library, she took a seat near to the window where she had a good view of the visitors.

Jeremy Thwaite wasn't as tall as his captain and he was a few years younger. His light brown hair, neatly clipped, covered a largish head, broader than average.

His face was round, his nose well-shaped, and his eyes large. She thought that they might be light hazel in shade, but she could not be sure without closer inspection. In all, he had a somewhat top-heavy appearance about him in view of his lean frame.

When Middleton entered with a large silver tray, the admiral grinned. "Ah! It appears the battle must cease for the consumption of tea. What a pity, I was enjoying myself."

"Papa, I didn't mean to interrupt your naval tactics—"

"You are not. Come and see. As these brave fellows fought in the battle, they have the benefit of first-hand knowledge. Mark the positions of the vessels just after noon." He pointed to several of the wedges. "See! Our fleet is passing through the enemy's line. The *Culloden* tacks to engage the Spanish to windward. Here's Quentin's frigate, exchanging fire with a Spanish two-decker as she passes the rear of our line. First rate! What do you say?"

Bella looked at the two younger men. "Your knowledge of that glorious St. Valentine's Day will occupy my father for many a long hour, and I thank you for it. But fighting mock battles will not stop hot water from cooling. Perhaps I can tempt you to tea?"

She left them standing around the square library table as she moved across the room towards the kettle and teapot.

Mr. Thwaite came to her first. "I trust you do not find our conversation boring, Miss Richmond?"

She smiled. "Not in the slightest, although I sense it's you who finds my interest in naval warfare out of the ordinary."

"You must forgive me, am I so transparent?"

"No, Lieutenant, you're not. I'm afraid the fault is mine for believing all naval officers assume ladies are not interested in their exploits. I judged you likewise, hence *you* must forgive me."

"We have underestimated each other, perhaps if we declared a truce?"

"Truce? What an abominable word!" The admiral joined them accompanied by Quentin. "Are you in favour of the peace, Thwaite?"

"Not in favour, sir, but glad of the respite."

"Respite, he calls it. Some respite!" Quentin shook his head. "Did you know this fellow is soon to be wed?"

"I definitely wouldn't describe marriage as a respite." The admiral laughed and turned to his daughter. "Did you know the Lieutenant was engaged?"

"Papa, you know I don't listen to gossip. However, as Lieutenant Thwaite only arrived yesterday, how could his news have preceded him?" She hoped she sounded convincing, she didn't want to betray her friend's source in London.

"That, my dear, only the neighbourhood can answer. While you're no carrier of tittle-tattle, I daresay news of the brave lieutenant is already circulating around the vicinity."

"Then the neighbourhood will have to call me plain Mr. Thwaite. As my father's heir, I have resigned my commission."

The admiral sighed. "Pity. England will need men like you to defeat Bonaparte."

While the gentlemen talked, Bella prepared the tea. When Quentin stepped forward, she asked him whether he preferred his strong or weak.

"Strong please," he replied, "without milk." Carefully, she poured the hot beverage into a cup, but it took all her concentration to ensure she didn't spill any. As she handed him the cup, his hand briefly touched hers sending a tingling sensation the length of her arm. Inwardly she tried to dismiss the feeling and pretend it hadn't happened. But to her embarrassment, she felt her cheeks flush. Quickly, she turned away, anxious to conceal her reaction.

"Miss Richmond."

Unable to ignore him, she turned back to brave out his gaze. "Captain Quentin."

She caught his eyes, their blueness contrasted with his dark, nearly black hair. Over the past few days, she had dwelled at length on his features and composed brief descriptions for her journal. She had written about his high forehead, straight nose, generous mouth, and, most attractive of all, his dimpled chin. Each time she wrote about him, she concluded that he was a very attractive man. His smile gave her joy, his eyes were so engaging sometimes it was hard to look away, and his complexion, she had noted, was especially good for a sailor. However, as she grew to know him better, her feelings for Captain Quentin had become deeper than just admiration for his features.

"I've received an invitation to Lady Mary's summer ball. Will it be well attended?" He asked.

"Most certainly, although Penley Court isn't a large mansion, it does boast an excellent ballroom. I wouldn't be surprised to meet half the county there."

The captain raised his eyebrows. "Then I very much hope you will reserve a dance for me, Miss Richmond. With so many people in attendance I'm sure you will be in demand."

"On the contrary Captain Quentin, I believe you will be the one everyone will wish to meet. So, do not be surprised if I hold you to your promise when the dances are called."

＊＊＊＊

It was a further week before Admiral Richmond relented and allowed his daughter to ride out. He had reluctantly given his permission after he had been satisfied that she had fully recovered from the carriage incident and all possible measures for her safety had been taken. She could resume riding but never alone.

During the weeks she had been forbidden to ride, Bella had yearned for the exhilarating feeling of fresh air in her lungs. Accompanied by Pride, she took her usual path towards the boundary of the Witton estate, where she drew rein to take in her favourite view along the river valley.

The early morning dew still clung to the foliage, making the tips of the leaves glisten in the sunshine. She breathed deeply, savouring the country air. With luck, she might detect a hint of the sea on the breeze.

Thin trails of smoke rose from the tall chimneys of Aston Grange and drifted along the valley. She couldn't resist thinking of Quentin and wondered what he might be doing. The thud of galloping hooves approaching curtailed her enjoyment of the moment. Anxiously she turned to Pride. "Do you recognize the rider?"

"It could be Captain Quentin." Cautiously he reached for his side-arm. He stood tall in his stirrups for a few moments.

Bella gazed hopefully in the direction of the rider. The horse, a tall hunter, looked like Quentin's and the square-shouldered figure could be him. Silently she wished she had her father's glass. "It is the captain, isn't it?"

"Yes, Miss, it is." Pride sank back into his saddle and made safe the double-barrelled weapon.

Grateful for the warning before he reined in, Bella composed herself.

"Good morning, Miss Richmond." His face creased with a broad smile as he tipped his hat.

"Good morning, Captain Quentin." Her heart leapt as she spoke.

"I trust I find you in good health? And your father?"

Unfamiliar nervousness coupled with exhilaration from seeing him gripped her. How could one individual create such havoc with her feelings? "Stand witness yourself, I am in excellent health and so is my father. But I owe you an apology. I would have spoken to you before, however, the matter is of a private nature."

His dark eyebrows knitted. "Miss Richmond, I'm sure you have nothing to apologize to me for."

"Indeed I do, sir. I very much regret inflicting myself upon you during our first meeting. The conditions you found me in, not to mention the state of my apparel, were…I smelt like a farmyard. I am truly sorry."

"You are too harsh upon yourself. Your circumstances were not your fault."

"That may be so, but would you kindly accept my most humble apologies and put me out of my misery?"

"Apology accepted," he nodded.

Bella expected her nervousness to ebb once she had spoken to him but the tingling sensation which had begun in her stomach burgeoned into a tangled knot.

She tried to keep their conversation matter-of-fact. "Sir Humphrey must be pleased to have your tenancy. It must be five or six years since he's been to the estate."

"I don't have his acquaintance, but the estate is to my satisfaction."

"Good news indeed." She checked herself. "For the neighbourhood I mean."

Quentin raised a questioning eyebrow. "Did you ride most mornings? I mean before—"

"Papa calls it the *carriage incident*," she cut in, aware that her body heat was rising. "I've always tried to ride, unless the weather was too inclement. Here, along the boundary between the two estates is one of my favourite paths."

"Hmm…you have good taste, Miss Richmond." He gazed at the sweep of the land before him before returning his eyes to hers. "I was wondering, there's a matter, if I may be so bold—"

The hunter snorted and Quentin stopped speaking while he patted the horse's neck in an attempt to calm him, but the animal began shifting his hindquarters. An experienced horsewoman herself, Bella recognized the creature's plight; the hunter wanted to gallop. Her mare, too, began to react to the stallion's unease.

"I would like your opinion on a certain matter," the captain continued.

The idea she might be useful to him intrigued her. "How can I help?"

"Possibly you would understand better than most, your father being a naval officer. I've been at sea a long time, and it is difficult to adjust to the customs and ways of the land. Since returning to England, I have found people to be most generous. In truth, I have received more visits from neighbours than I believe I deserve. Invitations, too, have been plentiful. However, I cannot possibly attend all of them."

Bella smiled. Lady Mary had predicted Quentin's popularity; however, it was slightly amusing that he hadn't. "You cannot blame the neighbourhood for wishing to welcome one of our naval heroes into our homes. We owe much to men like you and, therefore, we want to show our gratitude to those prepared to go to war on our behalf."

"There's no need to flatter me—" He broke off as his horse stepped sideways and he grasped the reins.

"That was not my intention. I was merely attempting to explain your popularity. Lady Mary says she has never had so many responses to her invitations. Why, some guests are returning from London especially to attend."

"Then I must not disappoint her."

She leaned forwards and gave Merriweather a comforting pat. "I have every confidence you won't. Captain Quentin, perhaps it would be wise if we dismounted?"

Quentin swung out of his saddle and tied the stallion to a nearby sapling. Pride dismounted, secured his horse, and then held the mare's bridle while the captain helped Bella down.

She loosened her foot from the stirrup. Quentin's strong hands circled her waist and lifted her down. Although her feet were on the ground, she thought he held her a fraction longer than was necessary. She was so close to him that she inhaled the pleasant aroma of gentleman's cologne on a freshly shaved jaw. An odd feeling spread within her, tingling softly at first, before rising to a crescendo and stretching the full length of her spine. She looked up at him and was about to speak when Merriweather neighed, tore her reins from Pride's grip, and reared.

Quentin's strong arms pulled her towards him. Crushed against his muscular body, she felt the full impact of a male torso. Her breasts squashed hard against the solid wall of his chest.

Shocked by Merriweather's behaviour, Bella took comfort in Quentin's embrace but worried over her usually quiet horse.

Pride failed to quell the mare and she continued to pound the ground and neigh wildly. "Keep back, Miss. It's the stallion, Captain Quentin, he's spooking her." He made another grab for her reins. Once more the mare was too strong for him. She wrenched herself free, bolted across the meadow, and disappeared into the woods.

"Take my horse and go after her," Quentin said to Pride.

"With respect, nay, sir. It's him that's sparked her. When I catch up with her, I'll not be able to control them both. The mare's coming into season. Begging your pardon, Miss, I shouldn't have let you take her out."

Simultaneously Bella and the captain realized they were still embracing and both backed off, embarrassed by their closeness.

Quentin coughed. "Take my horse, Miss Richmond, I'll ensure your mare is caught and returned to you."

"Thank you, but I can only ride side-saddle." She turned to Pride. "It appears my morning ride has turned into a walk. Let's hope we can reach home before Merriweather."

Quentin stared back at her in amazement. "You are walking back to Witton! It's some distance."

"Only two miles. If we go by way of the village, it's a mere stretch of the legs."

"Miss Richmond, I can't possibly allow you to walk—"

"Captain Quentin, we were discussing conventions on land. I can't ride either your horse or Pride's. And although Pride didn't admit it, my father gave him strict instructions never to leave me alone. But I can choose to walk home under Pride's protective eye. Perhaps you would accompany me?"

"Of course." With Bella at his side, Quentin led his mount as they walked towards the village of Aston. Pride, also leading his mount, followed behind.

"I don't know what came over Merriweather," Bella shrugged. "Usually, she's a calm, well-tempered mare."

"Perhaps she doesn't like being courted by Warrior?" Quentin gave the stallion an affectionate pat on his nose.

"Possibly, but she'd have to go a long way to find better stock. He's a fine example of horseflesh. Did you buy him locally?"

"No, he's from my father. I called upon him as soon as I arrived in England. He's resigned his commission and is reducing the size of his stables."

"Was he a navy officer?"

Quentin shook his head. "A colonel in the Royal Artillery, but since his re-marriage, he's every inch the country squire. The stallion was bred for hunting, not the plough. Finding myself on shore I needed a good mount, so my father let me have him, although he did hint he would like to use him for stud from time to time."

"Warrior is a fine animal. Obviously, Colonel Quentin is a good judge of horseflesh. But tell me, did he re-marry recently?"

"Two years ago, but I was a sea and unable to attend the ceremony. Being turned on shore gave me the opportunity to meet my new step-mother."

"How did you find her?"

"I am pleased to say in good health. She is a very kindly lady who appears to be very fond of my father."

"Your generosity does you credit, Captain. There are many men in your situation who would resent an ageing parent finding happiness in marriage."

"If she can give him some comfort in his later years, then so be it."

Soon they were out of the woods and walking along the road which led into the village.

"Would you?" he asked. "No, forgive me, I am too bold."

"Too bold to say what?"

"At sea," he paused, as if to gather his words carefully, "we grow accustomed to the ways of the navy. Sometimes we drift away from acceptability in polite society. I am used to plain speaking. Ashore, I must learn to curb my tongue."

"Have no fear. I'm an admiral's daughter, and if I had been born a boy, doubtless I may have been standing alongside your good self, or another captain, with a decade of service at sea behind me. I am not easily offended."

With each step, they drew nearer to the village and faced the possibility of meeting with acquaintances. Bella looked over her shoulder to ensure Pride was still close behind them. In her heart she wanted to remain with the captain for as long as possible.

"If the admiral were to remarry, how would you feel?"

The question surprised her. "My father has never mentioned or hinted at the prospect. Thus, I have no notion how I might react. However, I suspect my father's choice would also be to my liking. We have similar traits. I doubt if he would select a hoyden as my future step-mother."

"Would it be awkward for a house to have two mistresses?"

Bella thought his question slightly odd but decided to reply as best she could. "The answer rests with the two ladies involved. However, I could imagine a fraught situation arising."

"But you would wish your father to have some domestic comfort in his final years?"

"Most certainly, but matrimony may not be the best course for him. He can be very trying, especially when he's gripped by the gout. The lady would require a very patient disposition."

The captain laughed. "Few men make good patients. From our brief acquaintance, I believe you have the highest regard for your father and would not stand in his way if he chose domestic felicity. You are a very devoted daughter."

She looked up at him coyly. "Now you are flattering me, Captain Quentin. Although few of us are immune to praise, I doubt I deserve it."

"You're too severe upon yourself, Miss Richmond. You dutifully played me at chess, although I believe you were reluctant to do so. You obeyed your father's command and gave me a sound hammering."

"Ah! I wondered when our slight debacle would arise again." She was glad of the opportunity to discuss the chess game, but thought it too provocative to raise the subject herself. "Am I correct in assuming defeat is not a word in your vocabulary?"

"In my life, it cannot be. If my men thought for one instant I would surrender, how could I expect them to follow me into a fight?"

She noted his tone had become serious but couldn't help teasing him a little. "And you didn't lose the first game to me intentionally?"

He shook his head. "I wasn't concentrating fully and paid the price for underestimating my opponent's skill. You didn't spare me, Miss Richmond. Quite rightly. And I respect you greatly for it."

"And the second game?"

"I gave it my all and still you were triumphant. I have learned my lesson, not to engage you in chess again."

"So if you can't win, you won't play?"

He turned towards her, lowering his head slightly. "At sea, if I sighted a French frigate, she might carry more firepower than me. With seamanship and good gunnery, I might be able to take her. Two or three French frigates? Then I'd put up every inch of canvas I had and hope to outrun them. I must know I have a fighting chance before I make a challenge."

Bella didn't quite understand his meaning. Was he talking simply about playing chess, or was he implying that as a man he needed encouragement? Perhaps he disliked losing in any aspect of his life?

They walked on in silence towards the village and passed a row of cottages on the outskirts.

"Oh! Mrs. Winters is coming out of the end cottage. She will not let us pass without speaking." Bella felt her heart sink; the very last person she wanted to meet was the parson's wife. But more importantly, it meant her conversation with Quentin was over.

Clad in a grey cape and bonnet and carrying a large basket over her arm, Mrs. Winters waved and hurried towards them.

Quentin tipped his hat to her. "Good morning, Mrs. Winters."

She responded formally and eyed Bella's riding habit. "Is there something the matter, Miss Richmond? Where is your mount?"

Briefly Bella explained what had happened, tactfully omitting why Merriweather had been frightened by the stallion. "As you can see, we are walking home and Captain Quentin kindly offered to escort me."

Mrs. Winters appeared to accept the explanation without further question. "Lady Mary's summer ball is the talk of the neighbourhood. I do hope you'll be attending, Captain Quentin?"

"Indeed I shall, Mrs. Winters, and I am anticipating it eagerly." He glanced at Bella. "I've been trying to persuade Miss Richmond to save me a dance, but I don't think she's made up her mind yet."

"I'm sure I shall find a place for you on my dance card, Captain Quentin." And for Mrs. Winters benefit, she gave him one of her best smiles in payment for teasing her.

"How delightful. How lovely," clucked Mrs. Winters, "to have such a fine officer living in the neighbourhood. And so charming to have met you both this bright morning."

As they spoke, the blacksmith's boy came down the road leading Merriweather. Pride went to speak to him, took the reins and tipped the boy a coin. Having made her farewells to both Mrs. Winters and Captain Quentin, Bella remounted and set off homewards accompanied by her groom, as she had started out that morning. As she turned and waved to them from the end of the high street, she knew the parson's wife would ensure all her news was circulated before luncheon. As for Captain Quentin, she felt delighted to have spent time in his company.

As Bella rode back to Witton, she couldn't stop her thoughts from wandering. Her recollections usually occurred when she was in bed, during those few moments when slumber eludes the active mind. Most nights she relived the moment when his hand had glanced over her fingertips and the way his blue eyes sparkled when he spoke to her. Now she had the exhilarating feeling of being protected by his strong male embrace to add to her bank of memories.

She recalled how his protective arms enfolding her earlier that morning had reassured her. The joy she found in reliving those few seconds when she was pressed against his firm body surprised her. Remembering his strong arms around her, she wanted to be close to him again. Perhaps then she could discover what other secrets lay beneath his crisp white linen—*No! A well brought up young lady should not be thinking so!* She kicked Merriweather to a gallop.

****

Upon her arrival home, she left Pride with the horses in the stable-yard and walked across the garden to the house. Inside she found Lady Mary and her father sitting together in the drawing room, drinking hot chocolate. Quickly she explained what had happened. "With Mrs. Winters reporting our movements, the whole neighbourhood will know about me walking with the captain into the village. Unfortunately Mrs. Winters will have embellished every detail by afternoon tea."

"Perhaps if you stopped pacing the room and sat beside me, we could discuss this more calmly." Lady Mary patted the seat next to her, which the admiral had vacated. Bella sat down, and Lady Mary continued. "It's a pity Mrs. Winters has a way of exaggerating a tale every time she tells it. Undoubtedly she will give her intelligence maximum circulation." She smiled at Bella. "Thank you for informing us immediately."

"I didn't want either of you to hear before you had the particulars from me, especially if they had been embroidered in the telling."

"Fine fellow Quentin. Steadfast. Reliable. A good officer. He would make a very fine—" The admiral cleared his throat. "I've estate business. Now I'm satisfied you're unharmed, I'll leave you with Lady Mary and trouble you no longer."

Lady Mary offered him her hand. "Henry, you know I never tire of your company."

"Our feelings are mutual, Mary my dear." He took her hand and lifted it to his lips.

Bella was a little taken aback. She knew Lady Mary and her father were old friends, but she had not witnessed such an open display of affection between them before.

"Forgive me, my steward awaits my attention." And with a nod to Lady Mary, he quit the room.

Impressed by her father's gentle manner to her friend, Bella opened her mouth to speak, but Lady Mary spoke first. "This year my ball is proving exceedingly popular. I believe I've not received a refusal to date."

"Won't it be a rather crowded?"

"That's the cause of my concern," she sighed. "It's very vexing. With the London Season underway, I anticipated many people would have gone up to town. I didn't wish to disappoint anyone, so I sent out a large number of invitations."

"And you're worried your usual country ball will turn into one of those crowded London ones?"

Lady Mary bit on her lower lip, as if trying to think of a solution. "Do you recall your come-out? I particularly remember one ball, where there were so many people waiting to be announced, we queued over half an hour on the stairs."

"And once inside the ballroom, there were so many couples crushed together, there wasn't room to form sets."

"The disappointment those girls must have felt. A full dance card and no room to dance!"

"If you recall, I was one of those girls, although I don't remember being put out." Bella leaned towards her friend and whispered. "I didn't want to dance with the gentlemen who'd asked me."

"Minx! Do you remember how hot it was that summer? The evenings were very humid. So many young girls fainted, although I believe some did it for the attention." She paused for a few moments. "You did enjoy your season, didn't you?"

"Of course I did! And I remain extremely grateful to you for not chastising me when I declined my offers.

Many sponsors would have been offended when their protégés turned down proposals."

"Fortunately we were of one mind. Neither of the gentlemen would have suited you. It was so obvious that a blind parrot could have told you."

Bella laughed. She enjoyed her conversations with Lady Mary, and despite the age gap, valued her friendship. For Mrs. Winters and the local gossips, Bella played the daughter Lady Mary had never had. Lady Mary, in her turn, ranked as Bella's substitute mother. Both parties knew differently, as they enjoyed equality in their friendship, a rare occurrence between different generations.

"Chaperoning you gave me great pleasure and enabled me to re-enter society with the help of my brother and his wife. It pleased my family to have me restored to my 'rightful place'. My brother's words, not mine. But I've no desire to repeat the exercise. Give me a country ball any day. There's so much to be said for good food and pleasantries, interspersed with dancing and sensible conversation. If there's room!"

Bella had no time to reply. The admiral strode into the drawing room looking vexed, his high forehead creased. "The post has arrived. It's not good news. Your cousin is to grace us with his presence. He'll be here directly."

Chapter Five

Ross took pleasure in entertaining his guest at the Grange. There were times when he felt as if he was back on board his ship, in command of everything around him and enjoying male conversation. After a hearty dinner of roast mutton, they washed it down with captured French brandy from the *Diana's* holds. He missed the smell of the sea, the groan of the ship's timbers and the structured regularity of the days.

"Reminds me of our time at sea." Jeremy held his glass up to the light and gazed at the amber liquor. "How are you finding country life?"

"I'm enjoying it more than I ever imagined. The estate provides meaningful occupation and the local society is satisfying. I am more than pleased that I found this place, but it takes time to adjust to land."

"I know what you mean, old friend. My father would have me live on the estate once I am married, but I am having difficulty settling in the country. I would prefer to stay in London, if I were not harangued by silk and muslin."

"That is where we differ, Jeremy, for I did not like town. I found it smelly, crowded, and full of criminals."

"What? You didn't get turned over by footpads, did you?"

"No, but found a profusion of gambling in the clubs. I quit the place convinced that cheating was rife. I thought sharks were only found at sea. Sadly I was mistaken."

"You're wise to give gambling a wide berth. As sailors, we're too used to our own code of behaviour. In town, little control is exercised in the gaming houses. There are no limits for some rogues, and whole estates are lost on a single turn of the cards."

Ross frowned. He had spent the greater part of his adult life fighting the French and defending England. But on his recent visit to London he had begun to wonder why the place seemed so changed from how he had once known it. "Why, Jeremy? Why this madness in town?"

Jeremy shrugged. "Times are changing, we're at peace."

"The more I stay on land, the more I'm convinced that this peace is merely a ploy by the French to re-equip their fleet. The Admiralty knows it. The Government knows it. But everybody's afraid to say it!" Ross reached for the brandy. He was about to fill their glasses but stopped. A wave of sheer exasperation washed over him. "Damn it! I hope the Admiralty isn't caught fiddling while London burns!"

"Surely, Ross, it won't come to that. Have you heard something?"

"Sadly no. I've tried to convince them that a slumbering England will look ripe for invasion through French eyes. They refuse to listen." He removed the stopper from the decanter, poured two glasses, and offered one to Jeremy. "How did you find home?"

"Changed. I can no longer claim the freedom of a second son. That is why my father wants me to live on the estate. Now I am the heir, I must dance to my father's tune."

"Hence the announcement of your betrothal?"

"Precisely," he nodded. "I've never doubted Elizabeth's devotion. She has been my rock. Within weeks of my brother's death, her father gave his permission for us to wed."

"So having been initially rejected by her family, you now feel they are taking advantage of you?" Ross reached for the brandy decanter and topped up their glasses.

"Her father made no secret of the fact that the death of my brother had changed my prospects. His letter to my father was quite succinct. I had offered for his daughter and the lawyers would call to discuss the settlement. There was no mention of his earlier refusal. Did he have to be so crass?"

"Jeremy you are confusing tactics with strategy. Your attachment to the young lady was obvious. You were like a bear with a sore head for months when she turned you down."

"With respect, *she* didn't turn me down. Her family, the noble Glens, did!" Jeremy shifted in his seat and emptied his glass. "Our families had hoped for a union between my brother and Elizabeth. It wasn't to be. On first sight, Elizabeth and I knew we were made for each other. There was no objection from my father, and Elizabeth could have persuaded hers, given time. Daughters have a way of getting around doting fathers, don't they?"

Ross nodded and thought of Miss Richmond and her father. He had seen how fond the admiral was of his daughter and knew there would be very little he would deny her.

"Elizabeth's mother was a different matter. She wouldn't settle for anything less than a title for her eldest daughter. We nearly ran off to Gretna, but it was a foolish notion. We had nothing to live on, except my pay. And where could Elizabeth go when I returned to sea? You never allowed wives on board."

Jeremy's words stung Ross for a few moments. He had seen the sea take men's lives, depriving sons of fathers and wives of husbands. The sea had taken his mother too. The responsibility for his friend's unhappiness rested uncomfortably with him. "You know my feelings on that score. A ship is content without women."

"For some men it's a bitter blow to be single once they've left English shores. Yet for others, it's a blessing. As for Elizabeth, I couldn't steal her away from her home and cut her off from the life she was accustomed to."

"Your family? Wouldn't they have taken her in?"

"Aye, my father might have, but my mother insists on the proprieties. Eloping with my brother's intended would have condemned me in her eyes. No, I had to return to sea to make my fortune and pray that my beloved did not forget me." He paused and stared into his brandy glass.

Ross saw anguish in Jeremy's face and thought he had some great weight pressing on his mind. "My brother, James, didn't enjoy good health, and I miss him dearly. How do you think I felt when his death made me acceptable to my prospective in-laws?"

"You can't blame yourself for your brother's death. You *would* have married Elizabeth anyway. You said so, even if it was without her father's consent."

"Aye."

"So what's the problem? You can't bring James back, but you can find happiness with Elizabeth." Ross raised his glass in salute and downed the contents in one.

Jeremy's face brightened to a smile. "You are absolutely right. I thank you for your good advice and direction. But enough of me, Ross. How do you fare?"

Having replenished their glasses, Ross held the tawny liquid up to the candelabra to study its mellow hue. "I've been at sea since I was twelve. And before that, India. The peace has come at an opportune moment for me. I wanted land in England to put down my roots. This is a small estate and, at present, I'm only the tenant, although I'm sorely tempted to take the option to purchase. Aston Grange is comfortable, the land's good, and it's not too far from Portsmouth."

"Not too far when the fleet's pulled out of mothballs, eh?"

"Is my motive so plain?" He emptied his glass and looked directly at his friend. "We'll be back fighting Bonaparte before long."

Jeremy raised his glass. "For King and Country."

Ross echoed the toast and was about to down the contents of his glass when he stopped. "Jeremy, we are on land and must stand to toast His Britannic Majesty."

"Old habits die hard. Let us pretend we are at sea, eh?"

They raised their glasses to each other and made their loyal toast navy fashion.

"How do you pass your time in this haven you've discovered?"

Ross laughed. "The usual pursuits: hunting, fishing and shooting."

"Ensure, my brave hunter of the seas, that you do not become the hunted. You may think you have buried yourself in the countryside. However, as everyone in society has at least one relation looking for a rich husband, you're fair game this Season."

"Why does everyone assume I wish to take a wife?"

"It's the way of things, my friend, and I know you can be turned by a pretty face. Perhaps Cupid's arrow will hit you?"

Ross raised a cynical eyebrow. "I do not look to take a wife. I'm already married…to my ship."

Jeremy folded his arms across his chest and laughed loudly. "And the dear old lady is rotting in Portsmouth harbour with the rest of the fleet. The *Diana* is a hard task-mistress, but will she gratify your loins or provide you with sons?"

"You know damned well she won't, you insolent puppy." He emptied the decanter into their glasses. "Where can I find a woman to match the *Diana's* dash, style, and courage?"

"Now that *is* a new challenge for you. My advice is to start at Lady Mary's ball."

Ross drank the remainder of his brandy. "I thought you had an ulterior motive when you asked me to get you an invitation."

****

Bella and the admiral greeted their visitor in the library. Mr. Richmond bowed to his uncle. "Glad to find you looking well, sir."

"Granville," replied the admiral, his face displaying no emotion.

Next Mr. Richmond raised his cousin's hand to his lips, leered at her, and made his bow. "Dashed shame you haven't been in town of late."

"I prefer the country, cousin. Actually, I've not been to town since my come-out."

He stepped back, a look of amazement on his face. "Goodness cousin, why so long an absence?"

"I find little there to interest me," she replied.

He squinted at her. "Surely town has everything for a lady of fashion: fine warehouses, excellent seamstresses, and the chance to rub shoulders with the *ton*. Does nothing of that inkling take your fancy?"

"No," she answered sincerely and paused to smile at her father. "I prefer the country and, thus, choose to live here."

"Your future husband will indeed be a fortunate fellow," Granville said. "He will have the advantage of a wife and an estate, plus the freedom of *her* never wishing to be about town. The latter convenience alone must bring suitors swarming over your threshold. Am I correct, sir?"

"Suitors? Bah!" grunted the admiral.

"Then it is fortunate this estate is not entailed. If it were, I would inherit, and poor Arabella would find herself cast upon my good will. I speak theoretically, of course, for I know you have provided well for her, sir."

Bella couldn't decide whether her cousin was deliberately goading her father or simply resentful of his own situation. She suspected the latter. True, if there were an entail, Granville would be the beneficiary. The prospect sickened her. He looked so arrogant with his high stiff collar and waterfall cravat. But it was more than his appearance which displeased her. His pretentious nature tending towards the dandy, and his constant sneering at the world made him intolerable. She would not seek his company, if there were no family connection. Another aspect to Granville's character vexed her. Whenever he stayed with them, he selfishly helped himself to whatever he desired.

As a guest in her father's house, she had to be civil to him, but she remembered the self-centred way he always prattled on about himself. Innocently she had agreed to partner with him at her come-out ball, but was careful not to repeat the experience. The feeling had remained with her long after that dance. Afterwards when he did request a dance, she told him her card was full. Whenever they met at social gatherings, she created excuses to avoid him, if she possibly could. However, she had to make some conversation with him and asked, "Now we are at peace with France, have there been any changes in town?"

He lifted his nose arrogantly. "The peace has brought many fresh faces home from both land and sea. It's as if London's awash with officers. Some could benefit from the skills of a good tailor, if their pockets were deep enough. Those that have good apparel often have poor manners and too much money."

Bella wondered into which of Granville's categories he would place the captain. Quentin's clothes were well cut, his manners charming, and his wealth, reputedly, considerable. Probably, they would be introduced while Granville was visiting Witton. Although as yet, it was uncertain how long he planned to stay with them.

The admiral cleared his throat noisily. "I'm sure you'll not hesitate to help them part with the latter."

"Papa!" Out of the corner of her eye she saw Granville sneering as he picked up a book left on the table and feigned interest in the contents. Although she wasn't hungry, Bella was grateful when dinner was announced.

Numerous times throughout the meal Granville congratulated his host on the quality of his table and cellar. He consumed several glasses of wine. "I greatly appreciate you welcoming me to Witton, sir. It is always a delight to renew my acquaintance with yourself and my lovely cousin."

Bella raised her eyebrows, especially when he referred to her as *lovely*. Something was afoot. She thought her cousin's appetite was considerable as she watched him consume a large portion of the fowl and devour several slices of roast pork. The amount of food he ate made her feel quite ill. His gluttony was also apparent by his barrel-like appearance. Since their last meeting, Granville's waistline had expanded in the same direction as that of the Prince of Wales.

Admiral Richmond peered at his nephew. "Your visit was rather sudden, wasn't it?"

"Goodness no, sir! I wrote of it six weeks past. Did you not receive my communication?"

The admiral looked back at him blankly. "The only letter I received came a few days ago, informing me of your expected arrival."

"How very strange, sir, for I wrote a month and a half ago following a conversation with old Smythe, a small matter concerning my late father's estate. He was going through some legal papers for me and assumed I was your trustee with regard to Witton. When I corrected him, he became rather agitated and began muttering about your provision for Miss Richmond."

"Provision for my daughter is my affair. It is nothing to do with you or that meddling lawyer. When I die, my daughter will be well provided for."

Bella winced inwardly and took a sip of wine to calm her unease. The gentleman should have reserved talk of business to the privacy of their port and cigars. "Please, Papa, it is most disconcerting when you speak so."

"I have no wish to upset you, my dear. Whatever has been ordained for me has long been decided. I don't fear death. Indeed I might welcome it one day. However, not yet."

Granville nodded, his podgy cheeks shaking in agreement. His false expression didn't fool Bella. She had fixed his character years ago. He was not to be trusted. "As your nearest male blood, sir, be assured my services are entirely at your disposal."

The admiral looked unimpressed and offered no further words on the matter.

* * * *

Dinner preparations occupied Bella for most of the following day. Several guests had been invited to dine at Witton in the early evening. Bella busied herself by checking with cook, ensuring Middleton had drawn the wines from the cellar, and making sure the dining room had been cleaned and laid out to her satisfaction. She managed to avoid Granville at breakfast and took luncheon with her father.

"Your cousin's gone to Portsmouth, claims to have business with one of his merchantmen."

"Good, then he will not hinder me, for I find his conversation very verbose."

"And I find him diverting." The Admiral grinned. "I have to laugh at him, for it is the only way I can tolerate him for more than a few minutes. But I agree with you, every time he opens his mouth, he cannot seem to stop the words pouring out."

"The ladies will be few at table tonight, only Lady Mary and Mrs. Winters." She handed him the seating plan.

He glanced over it. "See you've got Quentin to yourself. I'd like to be at your end of the table tonight. Hmm…with your poignant remarks sandwiched between his directness and your cousin's verbosity, I'll warrant you'll have the better part of the dinner conversation."

"I have seated Lady Mary next to you because of her rank and I thought you might enjoy Mr. Thwaite's company too."

"Dinner will pass most pleasantly with her. As for young Thwaite, I like him." He rubbed his hands together. "But there's nothing like a bit of spice."

"Do I detect a little jealousy, Papa?"

"Nothing of the sort. I'm grateful I don't have to indulge my nephew again. Although judging by the amount of food the man can consume, it's a wonder he finds time to converse. But given the choice, I would like some of Quentin's conversation."

"You like him, don't you?"

"A man would have poor judgment of character, if he didn't like the fellow. He's a good commander. I've spoken to a few of his men and how a man is viewed by those beneath him, says much about him. Quentin's men are loyal. I've always found it prudent to judge men by their actions, not by what they claim to have done."

"Shall I change the seating arrangements? I can place Captain Quentin next to you if you prefer, Papa."

The admiral shook his head. "I believe Captain Quentin would rather sit next to you, my dear. As for my nephew, please keep him as far away from me as possible."

* * * *

"Richmond, how long do you intend to stay in the neighbourhood?" Quentin asked.

Granville looked up from his plate, glanced momentarily across the table at the captain but directed his answer to his cousin, almost as if she had asked the question. "With the Season upon us, I only intended to stay a few days, but with the prospect of a ball at Penley Court, I have been persuaded to remain. Then I must away to town."

"I'm surprised you were able to quit town when you did, cousin. In order to visit us, you must have refused a number of invitations."

"Family should always have precedence over acquaintance, cousin. However, there are some in town who will be disappointed not to find me there." He turned to Quentin. "I've been trying to persuade Miss Richmond to come to London this year, but she'll have none of it."

"You know I prefer the country to the town, cousin." She turned towards Quentin "I like the countryside and the sea. But if I had to choose between the two, I believe it would be the sea."

"Miss Richmond, would you place the uncertainty of the ocean above the safety of the land?"

"Indeed, I would, Captain Quentin. I like the smell of sea air and admire the strength of the wind. Fortunately, I don't get the sickness. But I would hardly describe the land as safe. Now we are at peace, there are stories afoot of highwaymen roaming the countryside. Haven't you heard?"

Quentin remained silent. His expression looked thoughtful, similar to when they played chess. A guilty twinge pricked her conscience for teasing him.

"Goodness, cousin, you've not been accosted by highwaymen, have you?"

Bella didn't want to lie, even to her cousin, but managed to shake her head.

A self-satisfied smirk spread across his face as he finished the last of the roast duck from his plate. "I didn't care to mention it upon arrival, but I had a slight run in on the way down from town. Not too far from here, four of the biggest assailants a man could face came bounding out of nowhere and fired at my carriage. I took out my pistols and managed to bring one of them down. The other three gave up."

"It seems we are all indebted to you for chasing thieves from our county." Bella eyed Quentin cautiously, hoping his thoughts were the same as hers regarding the similarity to their story. "I believe it's the very reason my father journeys by water whenever he can."

"I take after my father where sea-faring is concerned. He never did share his brother's nautical fancy, although he served as a mid-shipman for a time. I only go to sea when it's necessary." Granville signalled the footman to replenish his wine. "I can't abide salt beef and stale vegetables. A man might starve if he were forced on a long voyage."

"We do our utmost within His Majesty's Britannic Navy to keep our ships' companies well fed, Richmond. Men cannot fight on empty stomachs."

"Aye, Quentin, on that we are of one mind. Excellent fare, cousin. The duck was delicious."

Once the final dishes had been cleared, Bella invited the ladies to retire. She led them to the drawing room, where Lady Mary sat down at the pianoforte and started to play.

"Doesn't her ladyship have an excellent touch?" Mrs. Winters tilted her head to one side, as if to hear the music to greater advantage. "I am always pleased to accept an invitation to Witton, if only to hear your fine instrument. How long does your cousin intend to stay in the neighbourhood?"

Bella handed her a cup of coffee and sat beside her. "Initially, Mr. Richmond mentioned he would stay but a few days. When he heard about Lady Mary's ball, he indicated he wished to attend. Very kindly, Lady Mary has included him in her invitations. However, I doubt if he will stay beyond the ball. He wouldn't want to miss the best weeks of the Season."

Mrs. Winters looked impressed. "Does he have a wide acquaintance in London?"

"I do not know. He often refers to people by name."

"Oh, dear, I do hope he doesn't find us too tedious. However, with such illustrious company at the admiral's table tonight, surely he can't find us wanting?"

Bella knew to be careful what she said to the parson's wife. The news of seeing the admiral's daughter and the dashing sea captain walking together, after there had been an incident over the lady's horse, had been well circulated throughout the parish. "My father prefers to entertain men of his own ilk—in short, the navy. Whereas Mr. Richmond spends his time at his club with gentlemen of the town. I'm of the opinion that those two masculine worlds do not mix well together, but I have no evidence to qualify my view."

Mrs. Winters smiled as she nodded her agreement. "I've often wondered what the gentlemen find to discuss over their port and cigars, but Mr. Winters is always the soul of discretion, so I don't suppose I shall ever know. You must feel very honoured to have Captain Quentin's mark on your dance card."

"It's not a question of honour, Mrs. Winters, simply the action of a kindly neighbour." Beneath her coffee cup saucer, she crossed her fingers and hoped her explanation was satisfactory. "Captain Quentin is newly arrived and wishes to mix with local society. What better way than to attend a local ball? And doubtless he will dance with several other ladies during the course of the evening."

"Will there be an equal number of ladies and gentlemen in attendance?" Mrs. Winters asked Lady Mary, who had finished playing her piece and crossed the room to join them.

"I won't know until I've received all the replies. However, with a larger number of naval officers in the neighbourhood, I believe there may be more gentlemen."

Obviously delighted, Mrs. Winters clapped her hands. "How wonderful! What a pleasant arrangement."

Chapter Six

When they arrived back at the Grange, Ross asked, "Are you out of sorts Jeremy? You appear unusually melancholy this evening. Missing Elizabeth?"

"Naturally I feel the loss of her company keenly, but someone else is vexing me—Granville Richmond. I've seen him before."

"And he gives you cause for concern?" They settled in armchairs on either side of the hearth in Ross's study.

"I believe so, but before I tell you the whole story, from whom do you lease the Grange?"

Ross handed his friend a glass of brandy. "Sir Humphrey Westwood."

Jeremy took the drink and let out a long breath. Then he leaned forwards, elbows on knees, and cradled the glass in his hands. "I might have guessed. A month ago, after we'd been paid off, I was at my club and witnessed a card game. The first player, an elderly gentleman, picked up the card dealt to him. His hands shook. Stakes were high. 'Too much for me,' he declared and threw in his hand. A substantial pot had accumulated. Promissory notes and gold coins piled high in the centre of the gaming table. On-lookers gathered around, eager to see the final stages of a high-stakes game. The atmosphere reminded me of our weeks becalmed in the Tropics, close and humid."

"And Richmond's involvement?"

"He was one of the players. Another was Sir Humphrey Westwood."

"Are you sure it was Sir Humphrey?"

Jeremy nodded. "He's an acquaintance of my father. He lost his wife and eldest son a few months ago, so I didn't expect to see him in town gambling. He was heavily into the game, and he wrote out another note and slapped it on the table. Richmond raised the stake to ten thousand. Onlookers gasped and the next player dipped out."

Ross sighed. "That old ploy? Get rid of the parties, one by one, and then pounce on your unwitting victim. How could Sir Humphrey be taken in so easily?"

Jeremy shrugged. "I don't know. A murmur started to pass around the room about cheating. Sir Humphrey could have backed out and left his stake money on the table. But I doubt if he could have stood the loss. Richmond goaded him to quit, and when Sir Humphrey wrote another note, he said he would only accept it, if he put up one of his estates."

"Bait the quarry, and when the hook's in deep, reel him in. Didn't Sir Humphrey know he was being taken hook, line, and sinker?"

Jeremy shook his head. "I doubt it."

"What happened?"

"I watched the next player, curious to know Richmond's game. The man had a quiet demeanour. He matched the stake and raised it by the same amount each round. I watched him slide his hand along the table while Sir Humphrey argued the value of his collateral."

"And the outcome? Richmond can't have won the Grange, otherwise he'd be here grinning like a Cheshire cat."

"The quiet player moved his hand again. A footman in the Club's livery grabbed the man's wrist and riveted it to the table. The major domo declared the game null and void. All stake monies and notes were returned to their owners."

"Who tipped off the board of senior members?"

"Again, I don't know. Richmond got away without a blemish on his character. I suspected collaboration. I'm sure the man had a card under his hand ready to feed to Richmond. Once the original stakes were returned, he was allowed to withdraw his hand without disclosure. Honour was satisfied. I had forgotten about the incident until I met Richmond tonight."

* * * *

The next day when Bella arrived in the yard for her early morning ride, Pride doffed his hat. "Merriweather's to be stabled, Miss."

"What's wrong? Is she hurt?"

"The mare's fine, Miss. I've had orders she's to be covered today. A lad's bringing Captain Quentin's stallion over later."

The news surprised her. There had been no plans to mate Merriweather, although she was ready for breeding. Warming to the idea, Bella smiled to herself. Warrior was a fine stud.

At the clop of hooves on cobbles, she glanced over her shoulder. It was Watson, an assistant groom, leading out the admiral's horse already carrying her side-saddle. Pride helped her mount and together they rode out along their usual route.

The sun was breaking through the early mist as Bella led the way across familiar meadows towards the boundary of the Witton estate. Secretly she hoped she might meet the captain. However, she could think of at least a dozen reasons why he wouldn't be out riding this morning.

Her heart leaped as a single horse and rider galloped across the long meadow towards them. Instantly recognizable, the stallion's sleek chestnut coat glistened in the bright sunlight. When Quentin caught up with them, he tipped his hat as they reined in. Formal greetings over, the couple set their mounts to a steady walk and Pride followed behind at a discreet distance.

Although slightly nervous on their initial meeting, when he smiled at her, something special ignited within her. She enjoyed the way he looked at her. His blue eyes sparkled, and the dimple in his chin deepened when his face broadened to a grin.

"Thank you for the dinner party last night. The beef was particularly tender, and the ducks were very succulent. Please give my compliments to your cook."

"Your appreciation will be passed onto the staff. I am pleased you enjoyed the evening." She turned her head towards him and rewarded him with a smile. "I'd hoped to speak to you after dinner, but somehow I was prevented."

"Mr. Richmond eagerly claimed your attention."

"Indeed he did. After you all rejoined us for coffee, he scarce left my side. However, as my father successfully monopolized you and Mr. Thwaite for most of the evening, I can't blame my cousin entirely."

"And where is Mr. Richmond this morning?"

"I doubt he is ever about before noon. He is a town person who keeps town hours." She ducked to avoid a low branch in the small copse they had entered.

"Forgive me for speaking plainly, Miss Richmond. I do not have your advantage of a long acquaintance with the gentleman, but I have no desire to associate with him further. Last night I recall you said you preferred the country to the town, and the sea to the land. Is that true, or were you toying with Mr. Richmond?"

She smiled coyly back at him. "True with regard to my preference, however, I see you are an acute observer of character. On my cousin's account, I have no choice over the matter of acquaintance since he is a blood relation. When I see him he has a habit of raising the stubbornness in my character. He vexes me, so I remind him of the differences between us."

"Does Mr. Richmond visit regularly?"

"Fortunately he does not." Her reply caused a slight flicker of a smile to cross his lips. "My sentiments regarding my love of the sea were made in all honesty. It is a trait I share with Lady Mary. In many respects, we are of a similar nature."

Quentin straightened his back, having bent, like Bella, to avoid the branches. "Her ladyship is respected and admired in many circles, especially within the Service."

"Did you know she spent many years at sea with her husband?" When he didn't reply she continued. "She speaks fondly of her days at sea and claims her only illness was one winter when she was left ashore in Plymouth. Her tales of the West and East Indies are wondrous." Bella watched his expression tense and wondered if her words made him uneasy. She wanted to ask him why.

"Lady Mary sailed with her husband, thus she enjoyed the protection of his rank. Some officers regularly take their wives with them, usually the ones without children. Although I have known a few youngsters on board, generally warships are no place for women or small children."

His words made her heart sink. He shared the same views as her father, but perhaps he was more lenient with his officers than the admiral had been. "Did your officers take their wives with them?"

"No, they knew I didn't approve. Most officers hope to make enough to live comfortably when they return home. Only when a man can support a wife should he feel at liberty to choose one."

Was Quentin ready to choose a wife? Bella feigned laughter to hide her excitement. But she couldn't resist teasing him. "Forgive my boldness, but you choosing a wife is the current gossip of the neighbourhood."

"Really?"

"When a single gentleman settles into a neighbourhood, it is generally assumed he must want a wife." She watched him closely, keen to note his reaction and detected a slight reddening of his cheeks.

They had reached the top of the hill and halted their mounts. The view along the valley provided an excellent panorama. The mist had lifted, leaving the Grange bathed in the sunlight.

"I'm sorry, Captain, I thought you were aware of the situation. By accepting an invitation to Lady Mary's ball, the neighbourhood has cast you into the role of Perrault's prince. Every young lady in the county, and beyond, will be wearing her finest. Of course, you will notice the most beautiful, choose her, and live happily ever after."

"You don't believe in fairy tales, do you?"

"Thankfully, Captain, I do not. However, you have created a veritable squall in the otherwise calm sea of our country society by accepting your invitation. My advice would be to run with the tide. Many hopefuls will come to Penley this year full of expectation. Inevitably many will go home disappointed." She paused for a few moments and attempted to gauge his reaction. His amusement was evident, but was he diverted by her news and laughing at himself? She hoped so.

"I owe you much, Miss Richmond, for not only being my ears and eyes in the neighbourhood, but also for providing me with a source of entertainment."

"You had best laugh it off, for I fear you cannot run against the tide."

He raised his dark eyebrows. "Really? Why not?"

"If it is your intention to seek a bride—" Bella paused and glanced at Quentin. "This is purely theoretical, you understand?"

"Absolutely," he nodded.

"Once she is selected, the others will return home disappointed. However, the more you dally over your choice, the longer you remain the centre of attention. Ambitious mothers form a persistent army. They will continue to parade their daughters before you."

"Ghastly tedious," he frowned mockingly.

"Captain Quentin, you are not the sort of man who suffers from indecision; once your mind is made up, you must go to it! If marriage was not your intention when you decided to attend Lady Mary's ball, I'm afraid it's too late."

"Should I cancel?"

"Heavens, no! That would make matters worse. You must go into battle flying your true colours. It was not Lady Mary's doing. She gives a ball every year, although not one so well attended as this one's likely to be. She is as much a victim as you are. Now the runners make ready for the marriage stakes. The selected fillies, groomed to their finest, come under starters' orders. So I suggest you help Lady Mary clear her decks and prepare for all boarders."

He looked across at her, his countenance a mixture of bewilderment and mirth. Bella, too, was having difficulty suppressing her laughter, but the opportunity to tease him further was irresistible. "Don't you understand? Every available young lady in the county between fifteen and forty is about to cross Penley's threshold, albeit for one evening!"

"I swear, Miss Richmond, you are enjoying this at little too much."

She laughed. "Forgive me, but I couldn't resist teasing you."

"Your suggestion to help Lady Mary; she will not be offended by my interference?"

"I believe she would welcome it. I am calling upon her today. If she is agreeable, may I bring her to the Grange this afternoon?"

"It would be a pleasure to welcome you both. Pray tell me, Miss Richmond, for surely it is my turn to tease a little, do you include yourself amongst the nubile runners?"

Bella felt her colour rising. Quickly she glanced away, pretending her attention was taken by a bird squawking overhead. But she knew he would be too observant to be fooled by the decoy. She turned back to face him. "Inevitably the neighbourhood considers me to be; however, as I have had my London Season and returned home unmarried, I do not expect to be among the favourites. Will you assist me to remount?"

As they rode on, Bella felt relieved that she had made her situation clear to the captain, and she resolved to say no more on the matter. But teasing him had been a pleasant diversion. "Why isn't Mr. Thwaite riding with you this morning?"

"He left early for London but will return for the ball."

"I found him very amiable, and I know my father likes him, although Papa favours anyone who will indulge him with a mock sea battle or two. Does Mr. Thwaite play chess?" She grinned.

Quentin laughed. "As a matter of fact, Jeremy plays well. However, if I allowed him to be lured to a chess-board at Witton without making him fully cognizant of the likely consequences, I'd be seriously neglecting my duty to him as his friend."

"Will you ever forgive me?"

"What is there to forgive?" He shrugged his broad shoulders. "I fell for your father's ploy, but I shall not make the same mistake again."

His tone had become a serious one. It was her opportunity to learn more of his views. "Papa believes the peace will be short-lived, what's your opinion?"

"Bonaparte will not be content until he has consolidated his hold on the Continent." His forehead creased to a frown. "To secure Europe he needs command of the seas. To defend England the navy will fight to the last man."

Bella held her breath for a few moments. The thought of major battles with the French and their allies disturbed her. She knew the calibre of the navy and believed her father when he had said nothing stood between Bonaparte and England except the Royal Navy. Those men were brave, but she knew her thoughts would go out to their families if the peace was broken. "With the fleet at home, there will be many new navy wives this Season. What will become of them when their husbands return to do battle?"

"Like the rest of England, they must wait and pray for victory. If England is threatened again, our navy will rally to the call."

He sounded convincing, like a true leader of men. "My father says that once a man has the sea in his veins, it is hard for him to remain ashore for long. I hope any prospective navy wife understands her situation *before* she commits herself to what could be a lonely life."

Quentin's lower jaw twitched. "A man would be a fool if he didn't make his future wife aware of the kind of life he is offering her. Loneliness is a domestic matter between husband and wife. However, nothing in life is guaranteed. Is it, Miss Richmond?"

Bella had no doubt that when the call-to-arms came, he would be one of the first to answer. She admired his courage, but felt a great weight descend upon her, knowing one day they would be parted by his return to sea. "No, Captain Quentin, it is not. Shall we gallop?"

* * * *

Later that afternoon, Ross was delighted to welcome Lady Mary and Miss Richmond to the Grange. He came out to the carriage to greet them and offered Lady Mary his hand. She took it and smiled at him. "Thank you for inviting me."

"The pleasure is mine," he smiled back at her. He liked Lady Mary; she had a calming influence upon those around her and always seemed to know what to say.

When he helped Miss Richmond from the carriage, he looked into her dark brown eyes and wondered if she might receive his attentions favourably. However, he didn't know when would be the best time to approach her. They were neighbours, he enjoyed her company, and perhaps she could be so much more. He realised he'd been holding her hand longer than was necessary, so he lifted her gloved fingers to his lips and dropped a light kiss upon them. "Welcome to my home. I have assembled the crew, I mean, staff."

Miss Richmond smiled back at him and he let go of her hand. Did a man need more encouragement than that? However, this was not the appropriate moment. He must not neglect his duties as a host. Due to her rank, Lady Mary entered the house first. She gazed along the line of men, nodding her approval as she passed by.

Ross drew himself up to his full height, proud to see how well they had turned out to greet her ladyship. "Allow me introduce my butler, Mr. Sanders. He served with me on the *Diana* as sail-master."

"My compliments, Sanders," said Lady Mary. "It's been several years since I've visited here, but I cannot recall the house ever looking finer. You and your staff must have worked very hard indeed to make it so."

He bowed. "Thank you, my lady."

"Lady Mary has a large number of guests attending her forthcoming ball." Ross announced. "As Mr. Thwaite and I have been invited, I would like some volunteers to help Lady Mary's staff."

"Volunteers for duty at Penley, one pace forward," called Sanders.

Both lines of men, either side of the hall, advanced in unison.

Ross found the rest of the afternoon passed quickly. He began to enjoy the role of host as he guided his two visitors around the house. "Perhaps you would like to take a turn around the walled garden? I am especially pleased with the progress of the kitchen garden. Despite years of neglect, we have been able to gather some of the summer fruits."

The ladies assented, and since the weather was warm, he had tea set up on the veranda overlooking the garden.

"You've taken a large weight off my mind, Captain," Lady Mary said. "The extra staff will be invaluable. I had no notion so many people would clamour to attend. Of course, the fault is mine for sending out too many invitations. I do not comprehend what has happened to society this year. I fear the county has run mad."

Ross smiled. "If you were speaking of London, your ladyship, then I would agree with you wholeheartedly. My experience of town, having been away so long, was identical. However, we speak of the country, and I'm convinced your summer ball will be a delight. I look forward to it immensely."

"You are all kindness." She glanced across the newly cut lawn. "Now you have the Grange set to rights, it's a wonder you haven't had the idea yourself. It must be years since a summer ball was held here."

"The prospect of so many people descending upon my hospitality fills me with horror." He shook his head. "Ladies, I wouldn't know where to begin."

"Take heart, Captain," Lady Mary said. "Social gatherings are our home territory. If we were at sea and spotted a French frigate on the horizon, I doubt if we could deal with the situation as efficiently as you."

He chuckled. "Ladies, I'm convinced you would think of something."

"What would you do, Lady Mary?" Miss Richmond placed her empty cup and saucer on the table. "The scenario is most intriguing."

"You mustn't make light of it, Miss Richmond." Addressing both, Lady Mary continued, "I'd beat to quarters. The sight of a French frigate bearing down is enough to make a man's blood run cold. I'd put up as much sail as I could muster and make a run for it. All the years I sailed with my husband, we came under French fire only once. It was a terrifying experience."

Miss Richmond gasped. "Run for it? Surely not! I would order the sail-master to get me close enough to put a shot across her bows."

"Would you indeed?" Ross leaned forward, intrigued by the admiral's daughter's plan. He had never heard ladies discussing naval tactics before. "Fighting talk, Miss Richmond, but what if the frigate sailed faster and out-gunned you?"

"I'd take my chance," she answered, "and expect my gun crews to fire at twice the French rate. Once she was in range, I'd wager my rapid rate of fire would compensate for her potentially larger cannons."

"It might and I'm sure you would put up a brave fight." He paused for a few moments wondering if his reply, similar to the one he would give a young midshipman, was inappropriate for her. Nevertheless, he decided to give it. "Do not underestimate the French. They're fine sailors and do not surrender easily. With their long guns, there's a strong possibility that you'd be blown out of the water."

"Captain Quentin," Lady Mary said. "As we're at peace, perhaps we should content ourselves with how you can help with the arrangements for my ball?"

Chapter Seven

The Richmond carriage halted in the drive of Penley Court on the evening of the ball. "Why have we stopped here?" The admiral asked Bella and his nephew.

Bella poked her head out of the window. Turning back to her father, she said, "There's a long line of carriages waiting to alight. Lady Mary's guests are arriving early. We'll not be lacking for company."

"In London, a ball isn't worth attending if there isn't a crush." Richmond pulled a lace handkerchief out of his coat pocket and dabbed his forehead. "There'll be a decent card-room, won't there, cousin?"

"Lady Mary does not neglect her guests. If gaming is your desire, cousin, I'm sure you'll be satisfied with the arrangements." Richmond sat opposite to Bella and kept looking at her. She did her best to avoid his gaze, as he made her feel uncomfortable.

The admiral shifted in his seat. Bella wondered if his gout was troubling him but didn't want to ask in front of her cousin. "Did Lady Mary invite the entire county?"

"No, Papa, I helped her with the invitations and very few people declined this year."

The admiral chuckled. "All after the captain and his booty, eh?"

"Papa, have you've been listening to gossip?"

"I couldn't allow myself to be left out, could I?" He nudged her elbow. "I wouldn't miss tonight for a barrel of French brandy. It's going to be first-rate entertainment watching Quentin run the gauntlet in front of all those young ladies. What do you say, Granville?"

"Bees gather around a honey pot." He touched his nose again with his lace and sniffed. "He made himself a tidy penny at sea, I'm told, so I wouldn't be surprised to find he's got his sights set on an heiress. Fortunes run together when it comes to the leg-shackles."

Reluctantly Bella had to admit her cousin might be right. Whereas possession of a fortune might make Quentin very attractive to the majority of young ladies, it also gave him considerable freedom of choice. She glanced quickly at Richmond. This evening he was well turned out. His high cravat tied into an elegant fall and his dark green velvet coat well-tailored to his portly figure. But, in her opinion, the man inside left much to be desired. His condescending attitude and arrogant conduct vexed her. The carriage began to move and they progressed slowly along the drive to the house.

"Is the ballroom well-proportioned?" Richmond tucked his lace handkerchief back into his cuff.

"Yes, Penley has a large ballroom for a country estate house."

He looked unimpressed by her reply. "Then be a good girl, cousin, and reserve me a set, for I doubt if I'm acquainted with any of these country gentry. Don't suppose they get to town often, do they? And there's nothing as boring as a country ball where one's acquaintance is restricted. One has to be so careful who one stands up with. These country tabbies will have a man leg-shackled for merely talking to one of their lasses."

Bella didn't answer. He had leaned forwards and his knees were touching hers. She adjusted her cloak, so she could move her foot away from his. He was the very last person she wanted to dance with, but their close family connection prevented her from saying so.

"Of course Bella will promise you a set, Granville. It's the very least she can do for a guest in my house." The admiral tapped her forearm, his expression pensive. "Won't you, child?"

"Cousin, I'd be happy to open the dancing with you." She lied. Bella disliked doing so but was determined to feed him with flattery. "With your vast experience of town balls, we country folk look to you to show us what is *a la mode*."

The carriage halted and the admiral cleared his throat as they prepared to get down. Richmond smiled. If he saw through her patronizing remark, it did not show in his face. They entered the house and queued to be announced.

"Bad form for everyone to descend on a place at the same time," said Richmond, brushing the sleeve of his velvet coat.

Bella ignored his complaint and nodded at various acquaintances. She noticed whole families, some with four or five daughters out. She knew most of them but failed to recognize some of the younger girls, doubtless straight from the schoolroom at their first ball. Eventually they were announced and greeted their hostess, who was supported by her guest of honour, Captain Quentin.

"Good evening, Miss Richmond, you are looking very well." Quentin lifted her gloved hand to his lips.

Bella admired the way the dimple in his chin crinkled as he smiled at her. His bright blue eyes glistened like jewels. His dark naval uniform, undoubtedly his best, and recently tailored, looked immaculate. The gold epaulettes of his post captain rank were displayed proudly on his broad shoulders. His pristine, white linen and his dark, nearly black hair skimmed his gold-edged collar.

"The young ladies will not be disappointed with *Prince Charming*," she whispered. "I hope you intend to dance with several of them."

He smiled at her quip as he held her gloved fingers firmly between his. "Miss Richmond, I hope you will grant me the pleasure of the supper dance?"

"Certainly," she nodded. His eyes seemed to gleam for her alone. Her heart fluttered. The evening was just beginning and she could hardly wait for their dance.

Other people were making their entrances. Sanders's deep baritone voice echoed over the crowd announcing each guest in turn. The gallant captain had to relinquish her hand, but not before he raised her fingers and kissed them once more.

After making their welcoming addresses, the Richmond party mingled with the rest of the assembly. When the music struck up, Richmond stepped forward. "I believe this is our set, cousin Arabella?"

Why he persisted in using her full name, she didn't know. Her father called her Arabella only when he was annoyed with her. When her cousin did so, it irritated her.

They took their places in the set and were joined by other couples. The ladies formed one side, the gentlemen lined the other. Quickly Bella scanned the male row for Quentin. He wasn't there. The music struck up.

Having agreed to dance with Richmond out of obligation, Bella decided to keep the conversation to the minimum. Thus, he spoke first.

"You're looking very well tonight, cousin Arabella."

"Thank you."

"Blue suits you exceeding well."

Although she had had no intention of pleasing her cousin, she knew her blue silk enhanced her colouring to perfection. It had been an excellent choice of gown for the evening because most of the other young ladies in the ballroom wore white muslin, which tended to make her look pale. Hoping to rid herself of him for the evening, she asked, "Can I introduce you to any young ladies?"

His curled upper lip answered her question before his words. Without removing his eyes from her, he said, "I'm standing up with the most beautiful woman in the room, why should I wish to meet others?"

His reply disturbed her. Richmond was self-centred. He did not pay compliments unless it was to further his own ends. "You can't dance all evening with me."

"Would that I could, cousin, but I know you have other engagements. I'm for the tables. There's bound to be a few hands worth turning."

His plan to retreat to the gaming tables pleased her. At least she would be rid of him. Aware of his reputation as a gamester, she guessed the tables had a far greater pull on him than the ballroom. Due to his recent, swift descent on them from town, she suspected someone had called in his bills. Tomorrow she would speak to her father about him, at least to ascertain when he planned to leave.

When the set was over, he escorted Bella back to the admiral and Lady Mary.

"If you will excuse me, Lady Mary?" Richmond made a formal bow to his hostess and left them.

"Bella, my dear, everything is going splendidly, despite the crush. I've been warning your father that with young officers ashore this summer, he's going to have a hard task holding on to you." She tapped the admiral's shoulder with her fan.

Bella glimpsed movement out of the corner of her eye and turned to look. A young lieutenant, whom she had agreed to dance with, was making his way across the ballroom. He bowed to his hostess and the admiral before turning to her. "Miss Richmond, I believe this is our set."

Bella excused herself and turned to accept the officer's arm. The young gentleman danced well, and his conversation proved to be most engaging. However, determined to sit the next dance out, she asked him to return her to Lady Mary, which he did.

"The admiral's found a few of his old cronies. Once they start talking, you know they're best left to their own devices." Lady Mary drew her to one side and flipped open her fan. "The young lieutenant you have just been dancing with, he's very handsome and doubtless possesses charm, but be warned he is of small fortune and anxious to marry well."

"Should lack of a fortune make him a poor dance partner?"

"No, of course not. You looked very well together. But he's not the first, and won't be the last, seeking to marry where there is money. Indeed, I wish him well. But I wouldn't want him engaged to a close relative or friend of mine unless it was a love-match."

"Love conquers all, does it?"

"You know my thoughts, Bella. If you do marry, make it for love. I thoroughly recommend it. Now, where is my guest of honour?" She raised her lorgnettes to her eyes. "I wish I could see better. Who is that dancing with Quentin?"

On tip-toe, Bella scanned the ballroom. She spied him in a set with his attention fixed firmly upon his partner. Her heart sank. She didn't want to expose her feelings to Lady Mary, but she couldn't deny them to herself. A distinct twinge of jealousy niggled at her. The lady was very elegant, dressed in silver grey silk. Her hair was a soft shade of sienna and her features very fine. "I don't know."

"Damn my eyes! I never could see at a distance. I should know her, of course. What's the point of standing in a welcoming line if you can't remember who you've been introduced to? Whoever Quentin's dancing with, she must be making a few young ladies envious."

* * * *

With his attention fixed on Richmond, Jeremy followed him into the gaming room. A few tables were occupied, some by elderly matrons. Richmond avoided them and seated himself with a group of gentlemen. Jeremy positioned himself near the door. During the first few rounds of play, he saw nothing irregular, but picked up snatches of interesting conversation.

"This is such a pleasant part of the country." Richmond nodded to his fellow players. "Exceedingly fortunate for me, as I'll soon be able to call the county home."

"Connected hereabouts, are you?" The question came from one of the elderly players at Richmond's table.

"Don't you know, sir? I'm Admiral Richmond's heir."

To hear him claiming inheritance so close to his uncle's doorstep surprised Jeremy. Surely Miss Richmond was the heiress? The admiral had purchased his estate, so an entailment was unlikely. He stepped a few paces closer to eavesdrop the better.

"Aye, I've heard of you." The player opposite Richmond grunted. "I wouldn't count your chickens before they're hatched."

"Hatching, matching, and dispatching seems to be all the talk of late. Soon I shall be part of it as my uncle wishes to keep the estate in the family. We shall be celebrating at Witton shortly." He chuckled and swiftly sorted his cards.

Jeremy didn't miss the sleight of hand. Richmond fixed the trick behind his lace handkerchief, which burgeoned out of his elaborately embroidered cuff. He had swapped two cards.

On first reaction, Jeremy wanted to denounce the sly devil. How dare he cheat at cards under her ladyship's roof? Prudence held him back. How could he prove what he had seen? For certain, the two cards would disappear elsewhere. Richmond had probably used the trick on numerous occasions. And what would happen to the pleasant ambiance of Lady Mary's ball? He left the three players to their fate and hoped Richmond didn't push the stakes too high for them.

As he left, he passed one of the *Diana's* old crewmen dressed in footman's livery. He passed a few words with him and suggested a change of cards would be opportune. The man nodded, and Jeremy left to find his captain.

* * * *

The evening passed pleasantly for Bella. She had a good share of partners. However, each set she danced, she scrutinized the ballroom for a glimpse of Quentin. After the mysterious lady in grey, she hadn't seen him dancing again.

When the supper dance came around, she waited for him in a corner of the ballroom. Her heart sank with disappointment when he arrived with the lady in grey on his arm. His dark blue uniform with its gold embellishments of rank contrasted with the cool grey of her elegant gown. Together they made a strikingly handsome couple.

"Lady Fulford, allow me to introduce Miss Richmond of Witton Abbey. Miss Richmond, Lady Fulford is Mr. Thwaite's sister. Lord and Lady Fulford are my guests at the Grange."

Bella greeted the lady with the usual formalities. However, the joy she felt in knowing her true identity was immeasurable, especially as Lady Fulford was even lovelier close up than she was from a distance. They were joined by Lord Fulford, whom Quentin also introduced.

Bella's elated feelings continued to soar as Quentin took her hand, tucked it into the crook of his arm, and led her to the dance floor. There they were joined by several other couples and made up a set. The music struck up, and the corner couples moved to the centre, forming a star.

No matter how many couples danced around her, Bella only had eyes for Quentin. Resplendent in his dress uniform, his gold epaulettes glistened in the candlelight from the chandeliers above. His dark hair gleamed, and she wondered what it would feel like to run her fingers through it.

When the dance brought them together, she drank in the pleasure of having her gloved hands held in his. The touch of glove on glove felt very feminine against his male presence. A wonderful sensation of protective contentment flooded through her. As they formed an arch at the end of the set through which the other couples promenaded, she looked up at him and lost herself in his gaze. His pure blue eyes seemed to shine for her alone. Entranced, she couldn't tear her eyes away.

The music stopped. They remained at the end of the room, hand in hand, locked in each other's gaze. And half the county looked on.

Chapter Eight

The next day when Jeremy joined him, Ross was tucking into cold roast beef and freshly baked bread. "Take a seat, my friend. Some food?"

Jeremy sat down but declined to eat. He put his elbows on the table and cupped his chin in his hands. "I've over indulged. I'm grateful that Fulford got me in his carriage last night. Or should I say early this morning? I swear it was dawn when we returned. Something occurred last night at the ball, and it's troubling me."

Concerned, Ross stopped eating.

"Mr. Richmond likes to blow his own trumpet, doesn't he?" Jeremy refused the small beer Ross offered him and explained what he'd seen in the card room.

Ross listened intently and nearly lost his temper when he heard Richmond had been cheating. He took in a deep breath. "Are you certain?"

"I'm as sure as I can be. It fits his current run of play, doesn't it?"

Ross put his hand to his mouth and thought for a few moments. "Would you oblige me when you get back to town?"

"What do you want me to do?"

"Investigate Mr. Granville Richmond. Get an agent on to him. I'll pick up the tally."

Jeremy's eyebrows lifted. "Does this mean you intend to offer for Miss Richmond?"

Ross leaned back and folded his arms. While he had listened uneasily to the dubious card playing antics of the lady's cousin, his mind hadn't wandered far from her. He could not deny he felt attracted to her, and her position as an admiral's daughter should have made her a perfect choice for an ambitious officer, but how did he really feel about her? Strangely, he wasn't prepared to confess it, even to his friend.

"You don't have to answer. But if you are considering the prospect, there's something you should be aware of. It was something Richmond implied last night."

Ross looked up but said nothing.

"Richmond bragged there would soon be a celebration at Witton. He claimed that his uncle wished to keep the estate in the family. I believe he meant a match between himself and his cousin."

The idea hit Ross like a body blow. Momentarily stunned, he tried to brush it off. "No, that's impossible. Two more ill-matched people couldn't walk this earth!"

"All marriages aren't made in Heaven. It may be no more than a marriage of convenience."

"Poppycock!" Ross threw his chair back as he rose. It crashed loudly on the floor. "The admiral's far too astute to be taken in by that puffed up nincompoop, nephew or not. You said the man's a cheat, which means he's also a liar. He's probably short of funds to boot. Admiral Richmond won't sacrifice his daughter's happiness to that worthless toad!" He paced the room, his anger increasing with every stride.

Jeremy looked on, a slight smile hovering on his lips. "I can't see Miss Richmond partaking in any marriage plans she doesn't wholly condone. But perhaps she is being lulled into a potential marriage of convenience for her family's sake? She prefers the country, her cousin the town; perhaps they plan to never reside in the same abode?"

"Same abode! The man's got red blood in his veins, hasn't he? Could you marry a lovely girl like her and be content to live in a different house?"

Jeremy shook his head, a wry smile on his face. "No, that would be very taxing."

"Precisely! And once wed, wild horses wouldn't keep you from her bed, would they? Do you expect Richmond to be any different? Oh! Heaven forbid!" He dragged his hand through his wavy dark hair. "It can't be true. The source of this intelligence is the man himself. He's a braggart! Believe him and we'd believe anything!"

"You're taken with Miss Richmond, aren't you?"

Hands on hips, Ross glared back at his friend but didn't answer his question.

"I don't blame you. If I were not in love and near my nuptials, I'd find the lady a very attractive prospect. Indeed, Miss Richmond would suit me very well. Her father's an admiral of good standing, and she's an only child. She is lively and engaging enough to keep a man amused on a cold night. She has style, flair, and backbone, an uncommon combination in a lady. I would take her to sea with me any day, if I could find a captain who would allow us on board."

Ross looked at his companion with a knowing smile on his face, "Jeremy, I know your game. You think Miss Richmond has caught my eye, so you paint her in the best possible light, hoping to make me jealous enough to go hot-foot to Witton and make her an offer. You nearly-married men! Why must you push the rest of us in the same direction?"

"Because marrying the admiral's daughter is a damned good idea."

Unusually, Ross felt lost for words. He stood glaring at his friend for several moments. Eventually, he said, "You're probably right."

* * * *

"Might I have a word with you, cousin?" Richmond called from the gallery above the hall. "It's a most urgent and delicate matter."

Bella watched him descend the stairs. His rotund shape appeared to bounce on each step like a ball. When he reached the bottom, he approached her slowly, puffing out his barrel chest like a male pigeon.

"Shall we step into the library?" She half-expected him to complain about his accommodation or the manservant she had assigned him when he arrived without a valet. Whatever was on his mind, it would be said in private.

"Cousin, you are all kindness and consideration." He had a confident smile etched onto his podgy face as he indicated for her to lead the way. Once inside, he closed the door behind them.

"How can I help you?"

"Fair cousin, you will have noticed that my visit to your good self and your esteemed father has not been made without significant purpose. And today, fair lady, I am in the fortunate position to be able to acquaint you with my intentions."

"Indeed?"

"My presence bestows wondrous felicitation on your father's household. Once our alliance has been settled, there is no doubt that happiness and celebration will ensue."

Bella's patience began to thin. "Cousin, speak clearly. Fancy words do not impress me."

"Dear cousin, prepare yourself for the joy which surely must ensue. Think of the contentment we shall bestow upon your father, who can rest at ease with the knowledge that the future stability of his household and our honourable family name will be secured."

"Mr. Richmond, please make yourself clear."

"How much clearer can I be? Am I not totally transparent?"

Bella frowned. "No, you are not!"

"I know it is my uncle's dearest wish, as indeed it was my father's, that we be joined. The knowledge that your future is secure and under my protection should be sufficient to bring about your undivided affection and gratitude. My dear cousin, I recognize your character to be sometimes of an independent ilk, and I know you like to have your own way, but for the sake of family and the preservation of our good name I am prepared to overlook your minor faults and intend to make you my wife."

Bella was stunned into silence. Her pompous cousin had just made the most audacious and vainglorious proposal of marriage she had ever heard. Needing a few moments to compose herself, she looked out of the window down the drive.

"Might I suggest we are married in London? It would be convenient for me. However, the local parish church will suffice, if you insist upon it. My choice would be St. George's in Hanover Square. All the fashion, you know, and one does have standards to maintain."

"Stop this at once!" She turned back to face him, her hands raised as if she could push him away. "You haven't had my answer, and yet you are already arranging the church!"

His eyes narrowed, and his cheeks flushed. He pursed his lips. "But—"

"Listen to me. We are first cousins. No marriage, of any kind, will take place between us. It is neither my father's plan nor my wish. It is not going to come about. And that is final!"

He stared at her for several moments through the small slits which were now his eyes. His face had reddened. His mouth dropped open as if to he was going to speak.

Not wishing to hear anymore from him, Bella said, "It is customary for a lady to thank a gentleman for making a proposal. I thank you, but I cannot accept your offer."

He appeared affronted. "I was given to understand there was an arrangement between us."

"I do not know the source of your information, since I've never heard of this arrangement before. If you have been under the misapprehension that an *understanding* was made between our two fathers, then I regret to tell you that you have been misinformed. If the intelligence was abroad when I had my Season, why didn't you speak of it then?" She gave him no time to answer. "It is a fabrication. I do not wish to marry you and, therefore, I decline your offer."

"Oh, I see your game," he said. "I'm to be teased like a plaything and rejected because you have another match in mind."

"No one has toyed with you over this matter except yourself. You are deluded." His thunderous look might have made a weaker female quiver, but not Bella. "I do not intend to marry. However, if I did, it would be my affair and nothing to do with you, cousin."

"You forget to whom you speak. I am your nearest kin after your father. Be careful what you say to me. There may come a day when you will regret your verbal assault on my person."

"Do not threaten me. You have made your proposal, and I have chosen to decline it. There is an end to the matter." Not wishing to debate with him further, she strode towards the door.

He called after her. "I shall speak with your father."

Calmly she turned the door handle, opened the door, stepped through, and closed it behind her without looking back.

* * * *

When Ross was out riding the same day, he saw the admiral talking to his steward in the long meadow on Witton land. Both men were leading their horses. He galloped towards them, reined in, and dismounted.

"We're back to farming this afternoon, Quentin. Damned good party last night, eh? Can't remember when I enjoyed myself so much."

Leading Warrior, Ross fell into step alongside the admiral. "Indeed, sir, Lady Mary did us all proud. I was delighted to see you dancing a set."

"Couldn't say nay to the hostess, could I? Though I fear she took the brunt of it. I've never been much use on a dance floor. But anything to please the ladies, eh?" He nudged Ross. "I understand you're the main quarry in the local hunting stakes. According to my source, half the young ladies in the county have got eyes for you. Take care. They'll be calling with their hopeful mothers and fathers. I wouldn't be surprised if they're already beating a track to your door!" He chuckled loudly.

Ross didn't reply. He was flattered that he should be so much in demand, but he knew it was only his fortune and his reputation that attracted attention. He had no desire to fall for the first pretty face that crossed his threshold. Would it be too much to ask that someone might care for him? He liked Miss Richmond, he dreamed about her, and something inside him told him he would find no better match. But would she think the same?

They walked to the edge of the meadow, which afforded a view of the land at the bottom of the hill. "I haven't thanked you for sending your stallion over," the admiral said. "Bella was a bit miffed—"

"She didn't approve?"

"Only because it wasn't her idea. She's a sensible girl who knows a good piece of horseflesh when she sees it. Don't worry, she's quite happy now, and she'll be better pleased if her mare's in foal." He glanced around him, as if taking in the lay of the land. "How's the farming?"

"Aided by my farm steward and a few journals, my understanding of the land is improving. However, agriculture needs time, and I don't know how much I have. If war breaks out again with France, I won't hesitate to go back to sea."

The admiral looked up to him. "Well said, Quentin, but until that day you're on shore like me and must make the best of it. I'm trying to provide more arable land for the home farm."

"Do you need more?"

"My steward thinks so. Don't you, Walters?"

The man stepped forward and doffed his hat. "It would help boost the crop yield. Harvests have been declining in recent years."

The admiral nodded. "I don't know about the Grange, but I suspect you could use a few more acres of prime land, if you've got the labour."

Ross thought for a few moments. "Before the autumn, I'd like to drain a few acres in the south of the estate. I think there's underlying clay, since the pasture is waterlogged."

"What do you think, Walters?" the admiral said.

"If it's the land I'm thinking of, you're perfectly right, sir. I've got details of a new drainage scheme used in the Fens. I'd be only too willing to let you have sight of the pamphlet, sir."

Ross thanked him and asked to see the details of the new scheme when it was convenient. They walked to the edge of the land which the admiral proposed to plough. A group of his men were at work, and the steward took his leave. It was the opportunity Ross had been waiting for. "Permission to speak privately, sir."

"No need to be so formal, Quentin. I'm retired. What's on your mind?"

"Miss Richmond."

"Ah, I might have guessed."

"I've…I wondered if…"

"Spit it out lad. Am I correct in thinking you might be interested in her?"

For Ross, it marked a moment of truth. To hesitate might convey indecision or lack of feeling. Jeremy was right; Miss Richmond would make a good navy wife. But proposing to her required a type of courage he had never tested. He had no idea of her feelings for him. The more he thought of her, the more he wanted her. However, he needed encouragement or reassurance. He hoped that by getting her father on his side the course of true love would run a little smoother. He took a deep breath. "With your permission, sir, I would like her to be my wife."

"Hmm. And what's Bella got to say about it?"

"I don't know."

"So, you haven't made her an offer yet?"

Ross shook his head.

"She can be very obstinate. My daughter's character is similar to mine. We can be very stubborn at times." He looked up at Ross and smiled, "Don't worry. She has a good head on her shoulders. It could be a good match. But you've got to handle her properly. She doesn't suffer fools gladly."

"Do I have your permission to approach Miss Richmond?"

"Certainly, but anticipate a rough ride. She's had offers before and turned them down. Looking back at the fellows, I'm damned glad she did. They would never have made her happy. But you? Now that's a different matter. Mind, with every filly in the county after you, it might turn her head in your favour. Nothing like a bit of competition, eh?"

Ross knew he wanted a simple life. Society didn't hold his interest. After only two weeks in London, he had had enough of polite conversation, not to mention the stench of the place. Aston Grange had provided the safe port he needed and enclosed in its protective grounds, he had begun to feel at home. He felt comfortable there. When he wanted to venture further afield, the rolling hills of the surrounding county of

Hampshire, with their hint of the sea, had become his temporary haven.

"I wish to settle," he confessed, "and I believe Miss Richmond would be a good choice of wife." Ross felt the admiral's eyes upon him, searching his face.

"As her father, I must insist upon one condition: the final word must be hers."

"Absolutely."

"Then go to it!"

* * * *

"Miss Richmond? I believe she's walking in the garden."

Ross dismounted and handed the reins to Pride, who led Warrior to the stables. He felt uneasy and bit his lower lip. He had known the same nervous apprehension before, on the threshold of battle. As he walked down the path towards the house his stomach tensed with every pace. He found her in the rose garden. She looked up at him and smiled, shading her eyes from the warm afternoon sun with her parasol.

"Captain Quentin, what a surprise!"

"I hope surprise doesn't mean unwelcome." A warm feeling rushed through his veins as he took in her loveliness. How adorable she looked in her yellow dress. Her rich blonde curls, last night piled on top of her head, were now constrained under a straw bonnet which framed her fine features.

Two large brown eyes locked with his. "You're always welcome at Witton, but I didn't expect you to call today. There must be several demands upon your time. Have your guests recovered from the ball?"

"I believe so, but I have been about the estate so I have not seen them today. I left the Fulfords in Jeremy's tender care."

"I hope to meet them again, especially Lady Fulford. I found her most amiable and would like to know her better. Wasn't the ball an outstanding success? I sent a note this morning but didn't presume to call. Lady Mary will be far too occupied putting Penley to right after so many guests."

Ross watched her closely as she spoke, admiring the gentle tone of her voice, and waiting for the opportune moment. He had prepared a speech and rehearsed it several times over as he rode towards Witton "I enjoyed the ball enormously, Miss Richmond, and particularly our two dances."

"Thank you, captain, I too enjoyed the dancing."

"I had the pleasure of meeting your father this morning while I was about the estate." He had started to ramble and his heart began to pound. He needed a few moments respite. "Could we take a turn around the garden?"

They walked only a short distance, but he couldn't contain himself any longer. "Last night, when we danced together at the ball, I found the exercise very agreeable."

"The dancing was most agreeable. Attending a ball could be regarded as one's social responsibility, but rarely are they all as pleasant." She turned and faced him squarely. "I don't suppose you had many opportunities for dancing on board your frigate?"

"No," he smiled, "not unless we were in port and were required to attend functions with some of the local dignitaries and their ladies." He took a deep breath. "I do not think you are the sort of lady who would trifle with a man's affection."

He thought she looked surprised as she stared at him. Half expecting her to say something, he paused for a few moments.

When she remained silent, he continued, "Since I first met you, I've been moved by your loveliness, spirit, and ease of manner. Miss Richmond, I'm a man accustomed to straight speaking; would you do me the honour of becoming my wife?"

* * * *

Bella's stomach flipped over. Was the world demented? This was her second declaration in the space of as many hours. She couldn't reply. The silence stretched out between them, with only the soft sounds of summer gently vying in the background. What could she say? What answer did she have for him?

He stood before her, offering her his name, his fortune and his protection. Inwardly she was in turmoil. Part of her wanted to go forward, to grab hold of him, and to feel the passion of a man's kisses on her lips for the first time.

Yet something held her back. The blackness of uncertainty. Into what sort of life would she be leaping, if she said yes? For a long time she had protested that she would not marry and had refused to be moved on the subject. Now Quentin stood before her with his offer of marriage, but what did he really mean? Did he love her?

His eyes brimmed with eager anticipation. All she had to do was say yes. But did she risk too much? Once the first flush of nuptial felicity had passed what would their life be like? Would he yearn to be back at sea? Leave her behind for years while he sailed to the far side of the world?

"I...cannot answer," she whispered. "You ask too much...this is all so sudden."

"Forgive my presumption. I am scarce used to the niceties of drawing room courtship. I spoke to your father this morning—"

"You've already asked my father?" She felt a slight affronted by his action. However, she knew she would probably have censured him if he hadn't approached her father for permission to address her. Why was she so confused?

"Only for encouragement." Worry hovered around the corners of his mouth.

"You should have come to me first, for I have long professed not to marry."

* * * *

Her words were as clear as a cannon shot across his bows. A sabre blow couldn't have hurt him more. The appalling sensation of being caught in an awkward situation while saying the wrong words spread through his body like a plague. Could there be nothing more between them than neighbourly acquaintance? Is that what she wanted?

"May I ask the reasons why you have resolved not to wed?"

"I am mistress of my father's house, an only child—he needs me."

"Does he say so?" he asked sharply. Disappointment welled up inside him and threatened to burst into anger. He struggled to stay in control. "When

I spoke with him this morning, he gave no hint that your wishes were so."

"He knows me well enough, but I am not surprised that he said little of my opinion," she murmured.

He wanted to hold her, bring her close, and feel her body next to his. Perhaps then he could—no, he checked himself. She was the daughter of a man who outranked him. He could not take liberties with her. A tactical withdrawal to preserve his dignity, despite his severe disappointment, was needed. Several painful moments passed, and he took one last look at her. "I will waste no more of your time, Miss Richmond." He turned on his heel and strode along the garden path towards the stables.

* * * *

Bella tried to call after the captain, but no words would form in her mouth. Painfully she watched his tall, masculine figure disappear through the gateway. The dreadful knowledge that she had humiliated him stung her very being. Her face paled, as if the life she had in her ebbed away with every step he put between them.

The comfortable life she treasured began to taste sour. Proud of her singularity, like many wealthy spinsters, was she too proud? When she was eighteen she had rejected the marriage proposals from the peer with the lewd eyes and the older widower with the two children without a second thought. At twenty-three, she rejected Richmond's preposterous suit based on sound reason. That dismissal caused her neither suffering nor anxiety. But Captain Quentin's?

Her world collapsed around her. She had told the only man she wanted to marry that she had no intention of becoming a wife. What must he think of her now?

He had offered her his name, his fortune, his protection, and his love—what more could a woman want? For the first time in years, tears rolled down her cheeks. How could she have been so foolish?

She sank onto a bench, her hands covering her face. How could she have acted so stupidly? Why had she been filled with foolish pride? She had turned down the most eligible bachelor in the county, perhaps in the whole south of England. She could put aside his standing and reputation but not her feelings for him. In the space of a few moments on a warm summer day, Bella Richmond realized her feelings for Captain Quentin were stronger than she had ever felt for a man before. And she didn't see how she was going to put things right between them.

Chapter Nine

Ross threw his hat and riding crop onto the hall table and stormed into his study without speaking to Sanders or Jeremy. He poured himself a generous glass of brandy, glanced momentarily over his shoulder at his friend, who had followed him, and poured another glass.

"Are we celebrating?"

Ross scowled an unintelligible reply. With stiff body movements, he paced the room until he halted abruptly and glared at Jeremy. "I've been rejected." He threw the brandy down his throat, forcing the liquid into his stomach as if his life depended upon it.

"Ah, do you need to talk?"

"No!" Ross howled with the ferocity of a wounded beast and poured himself another drink. "What's the benefit of words?"

"Depends on the situation and circumstances. Get yourself totally inebriated. It'll help for a few hours." Jeremy raised his own glass in mock salute and took another sip. "But don't expect the bottle to cure the problem."

Ross turned on him. "When did you acquire expertise in marriage proposals?"

Jeremy smiled. "I've probably had more experience, and I also had my suit declined."

"By the family," Ross roared, "not the lady!"

"What exactly did you say? Females can be mighty sensitive to the manner of a man's proposal. Did you plan before you went into the fray?"

Ross replied with one of his direct stares.

"Of course you did. What went wrong? Did you make your feelings clear to her?"

"Yes!" He let out a long sigh of exasperation. "I said I had been moved by her loveliness, spirit, and ease of manner."

"Oh, dear."

"And what's that supposed to mean? What could possibly be wrong with telling her that?"

"Ladies like to be wooed. Surely something a little stronger might have been in order?"

"It's done!" He snapped. "When I asked her to be my wife, she said I was too presumptuous. As an only child her father needed her, and she had no intention of marrying. If that isn't an honest, straightforward, and final answer, I don't know what is!"

"No intention of marrying?" Jeremy frowned. "Did you speak with the admiral at all?"

Ross sank into a nearby chair and downed another brandy. Rapid thoughts flashed through his head, odd snippets of conversation from the ball the previous evening and with the admiral earlier, but one image remained—hers. "He couldn't have been more encouraging. But he warned me the final decision was hers and hers alone."

"So Miss Richmond claims she has no intention of marrying, which doesn't mean she's irrevocably set against you, does it?"

Ross looked back at him. "I wish I could believe you, but I'll not nurture false hope."

"She didn't say she was *never* going to marry, did she?"

"No," Ross admitted at length, his tone hardly audible as his senses began to dull under the influence of brandy on an empty stomach.

"Strategy, Ross. You must look to your campaign. Women are like vessels, they need careful handling. So what would you do at sea, if you'd just come off worst in a skirmish. You seem intent upon drowning your sorrows in brandy. Go ahead, I know how you feel. God knows I felt as sick as a dog when Elizabeth's father refused to sanction our engagement. Get yourself drunk. When you are sober, lick your wounds and plan your campaign. 'Faint heart never won fair lady' or something like that."

Ross raised his head. He didn't want to think of anything.

"I saw you dancing with her last night." Jeremy raised his voice. "What are you made of man? You two are destined for each other. If you really care about her, you will fight to win her over. She's no intention of marrying? Damn well convince her otherwise. Rise to the challenge!"

* * * *

Rejected by his cousin, Richmond ordered the carriage, so he might ride to the village. He had hastily written a note but didn't want Middleton to know its direction, in case he reported it to the admiral. He was furious that Arabella had declined his offer. He knew she was independently minded and, although he had anticipated her refusal, he craved revenge for the manner in which she had insulted him. He had plans for her. It would have been easier if she had agreed to the marriage. Now he would have to put other measures in place to get what he wanted from the Richmonds.

In the village, he chanced upon Reverend and Mrs. Winters and engaged them in conversation. Later, when he returned to Witton, he tried to get an interview with his uncle, but Middleton informed him that the admiral had ridden out on farm business. Anxious to catch him as soon as he came back, Richmond took up sentry duty at his bedchamber window, where he had a clear view of the stable yard and garden. From there he saw Quentin arrive and proceed to what appeared to be a pre-arranged rendezvous with Miss Richmond.

He watched from his open window and heard their voices, but he was too far away to make out their conversation. However, as Quentin left rather abruptly, he assumed there had been a disagreement, which pleased him greatly.

When he saw his uncle approach from the stables, he went downstairs to greet him in the hall. "You must be the first to congratulate me, sir."

"Congratulate you?" The admiral eyed him suspiciously. "Why? What have you done?"

"My nuptials, sir."

The admiral's high forehead creased into a frown. He removed his hat, handed it to Middleton, and turned on his nephew. "Why do I have the distinct impression I am about to hear something which will displease me greatly? If this is about money, we'd best talk privately." He pointed towards the library.

Richmond followed the admiral into the library and wasn't surprised when the old man took up a position against the mantelpiece. There was no invitation to sit, just a gruff demand: "What's afoot?"

"Wish us joy. Arabella has accepted my offer. Ever mindful of the proprieties, she wishes to keep the news to the family for the present. A formal engagement will not be announced until the settlement is agreed. However, I can give you the most steadfast assurance, Uncle Richmond, that I will endeavour to maintain our family's excellent reputation and ensure the prosperity of our estate."

The admiral's jaw dropped open. He shook his head. "Have you run mad?"

"No, sir," Richmond said. "The arrangement is to our mutual advantage. Be assured the future of your estate is secure. Arabella will continue to reside here with you. I shall take care of affairs in London. It seems a marriage of convenience will satisfy her for the present. A normal arrangement would be more satisfactory to provide issue. However, not wanting to be insensitive to my cousin's wishes, I'm willing to comply with her desires, as long—"

"Poppycock, Granville, I don't believe a word you say!"

"Oh, I believe you must, for on my journey through the village I stopped to have a quiet word with the parson and his good lady. As I told them, if Miss Richmond can be persuaded to town, St. George's in Hanover Square would be my choice for the wedding."

"Silence! Enough of this nonsense!" He rang the bell for Middleton. The butler entered the library a few moments later. "Summon Miss Richmond here immediately."

* * * *

When Bella came into the library, she sensed that all was not well between her father and cousin. Her father's thin face had turned puce. Worried about him, she went to his side. "Are you unwell?"

"I am fine." He glanced accusingly at his nephew, who was preening the lace at his cuffs, a self-satisfied grin on his face.

The admiral cupped her hand between his and looked directly into his daughter's eyes. "Your cousin insists that he has made you an offer of marriage, is this true?"

"Yes, father." She heard her father inhale deeply.

"And he maintains you have agreed to a marriage of convenience—"

"I have done nothing of the sort!"

Richmond leaned his head to one side. "Do you not recall our agreement?"

Bella pulled her hand away from her father's gentle hold and turned on her cousin. She advanced swiftly towards him, her temper rising. "We have no such agreement. We have never been pledged in marriage and we *never* will be."

Richmond stepped back, increasing the distance between them. But Bella wouldn't let him retreat so easily. She stared angrily at him, and his jaw dropped open.

"How dare you have the effrontery to spread spurious lies about the neighbourhood?" The admiral advanced across the room towards his nephew. "Did you think that by doing so, you could intimidate either me or my daughter?"

"No, sir," he spluttered, "but Arabella gave me to understand—"

"I gave you no understanding whatsoever," she insisted, "and still you have gone abroad in the neighbourhood with your lies. Your conduct is despicable."

The admiral frowned. "I am seriously displeased with your behaviour, sir. Your actions are not those of a gentleman. I insist you leave my house forthwith."

Bella wasn't used to hearing her father address another man in such an assertive manner. She wondered how many officers he had similarly dressed down throughout his career. There must have been many, since the service relied upon discipline and loyalty. An enormous sense of relief flooded over her. Her cousin was going, possibly for good.

"I am affronted, sir, to be treated so in your house and to be addressed by yourself in this way." Richmond lifted his head, pushing his nose in the air at his uncle.

The admiral refused to be intimidated by him. "What you have done is unforgivable. My daughter resides in the neighbourhood, where she is respected and admired. Through your selfish action and malicious tongue, you have severely injured her reputation. Go, sir, immediately, and do not cross my threshold ever again."

As Bella watched the colour rise in her cousin's face, she half expected him to continue arguing with her father. Mr. Richmond must have had an ulterior motive to propose marriage to her. Was he short of funds, in danger of being incarcerated in the debtors' prison, or simply a fool? She doubted the latter, but thankfully he didn't say another word. Red-faced, he turned, quit the room, and left the doors open behind him. She saw him climb the stairs and heard him bellow for a manservant to pack his bags.

The admiral came to his daughter and placed his hands around her upper arms. He drew her towards him until her head rested gently on his shoulder. "Do not fear, my dear. I doubt your reputation has been harmed by his fanatical lies. Anyone who knows your character and respects your good sense will understand that you would never allow yourself to become aligned with someone so dishonourable."

* * * *

Images and snatches of conversation buzzed around in Bella's head throughout the night. When the morning light invaded her room, she felt she had gotten no sleep at all. So much had happened to her, but she couldn't keep her emotions bottled up inside any longer. There was only one person in whom she could confide her true feelings about Quentin and her deep concern about her cousin's audacity.

Her anger over Richmond's behaviour had fermented overnight. If Mrs. Winters gave her tongue full rein, people would believe the cousins were engaged. Undoubtedly, that was Richmond's intention when he spoke to the Winters. The damage was done. How could she put the rumour down without compromising her reputation and good name? She needed help. She needed Lady Mary. After an early breakfast, she rode to Penley Court accompanied by Pride.

Lady Mary was at her breakfast table when Bella was announced. "My dear, you're about early. Please come and sit with me. Will you take tea or some hot chocolate? Perhaps a coddled egg?"

"Just chocolate," Bella said. She took a few sips before appealing to her hostess. "May I have a private word?"

Lady Mary dismissed the footman and maidservant. When they were alone, she listened as Bella explained the previous day's events, beginning with her cousin's proposal. "What a dreadful scene you had to endure, but how could Mr. Richmond be so impertinent? As soon as I see Mrs. Winters I shall correct the intelligence. Of course, the fault is not hers, but doubtless she will endeavour to perpetrate the news. But your father has acted correctly and sent him away. Let us hope we have seen the last of him."

"Indeed, but I have known him all my life. He's a bully who hates losing. My instinct warns me that we are not done with him at Witton Abbey."

Lady Mary sighed. "Enough of your cousin, Bella, he's not worth it. He has gone from the neighbourhood. But I can see you are upset, and I am not convinced Mr. Richmond is your only problem."

Bella managed a small smile for her friend. "How well you know me, Mary, perhaps even better than I know myself." She took a deep breath and explained what had happened when Captain Quentin proposed. Lady Mary listened carefully, her concern revealed in the lines around her face.

When Bella had finished, Lady Mary reached across the breakfast table and covered Bella's hand with hers. "What I don't understand, my dear, is whatever possessed you to tell Captain Quentin you had no intention of marrying. I know you have often professed that you do not see the merit of matrimony, but I thought it was an excuse you used to quiet the gossips and discourage any unsuitable gentlemen. You see, I never quite believed you, despite your claim. I thought when a suitable offer came along, or you fell in love, your claim to perpetual spinsterhood would be dropped. I thought that gentleman was Captain Quentin. I had it in my mind's eye that you, the admiral's daughter, and he, the dashing captain, were a perfect match. And I don't think I was alone in believing so. Thus, I do not understand why you told him you had no intention of marrying."

Bella let out a deep sigh, she felt utterly silly. "I have asked myself that question a thousand times. It must have slipped out. I don't know what came over me. Was I taken by surprise or diverted by the other ludicrous proposal I had received? Before I had time to reflect, he turned away from me and left. Oh, I wanted to run after him and tell him I was wrong, but I couldn't. Although he might make me the happiest woman in the world, I know there will be a day when he returns to sea and leaves me behind."

Lady Mary did not reply immediately. Eventually, she said, "You acted impulsively, didn't you?"

Bella nodded.

"And without realizing your true feelings for him?"

"Yes, I don't think I knew what I was saying."

"And now you have had time to think, what are your true feelings?"

"I feel utterly miserable. I love him, Mary. But I can't marry him, because he'll go away, and I'll be left…and I'll end up like my mother, pining for him." Bella felt a great storm of emotion well up inside her. Her eyes filled with hot tears which began to roll down her cheeks.

Lady Mary moved to her side and placed a comforting arm around her. "What do you think your mother would say if she were here?"

Bella raised her head slightly, and sniffed back a few tears. "I don't know."

"When I fell in love with Charles, and my father refused permission for us to marry, I thought it was the end of the world. I loved him so much, Bella, that I didn't consider what would happen when he went back to sea. I couldn't wait to be his wife."

"But you didn't have to wait, did you?"

"No, I was lucky. I was of age and so we made our dash for Gretna. We spent our honeymoon in Scotland. My parents refused to receive us after the wedding, so I went to sea with Charles."

"But Quentin won't ever take me on board. He's like my father."

"And having rejected him, you think it's final?"

Bella nodded. "He's a man of his word, decisive and proud. Rejection would not bode well with him. He's used to winning. Oh, Mary! What am I to do?"

"I don't know, my dear. But if his feelings are as deep for you as yours are for him, love will triumph. Believe me."

* * * *

The following day, Admiral Richmond's steward, Walters, reported the loss of several lambs during the night. "From the top land, sir, running up to Aston Hill. We've never had trouble up there before. I'd like to take a few guns out and see what we can flush out."

"Foxes?"

"Or dogs, sir. I can't be sure. There was no warning. If it's a hungry vixen with cubs to feed, usually one or two lambs go amiss. But there's half a dozen dead, ravaged, and not much meat taken."

"And the neighbours? Have any of them reported similar trouble?"

"No, sir, though I did have a word with the captain. He was out riding first thing this morning. He said if we needed extra men, he'd be only too glad to help."

Admiral Richmond ordered Bella to remain at home, gathered his men, and set off on horseback with his search party. Woods covered the top of Aston Hill, and the sheep grazed on the lower slopes. With beaters and dogs working together, they began sweeping the area, hoping to flush out the guilty party.

* * * *

Ross woke with a start and wished he hadn't moved his head so quickly. The inside of his skull throbbed so much he thought somebody had used him as a punch-bag. He tried to lick his parched lips, then remembered the bottle of brandy he had consumed the previous night. But it wasn't his physical state that hung heavily over him. He knew he'd recover from that, but would he ever find solace? He punished himself every time he thought of her and tried to force her image to the back of his mind. His fuddled brain would not allow him to do so. She was there on his mind, regardless of whether he opened or closed his eyes. He stumbled down to breakfast where he found Jeremy.

"We mean to take the London road with all haste. Will you ride with us as far as the turnpike?" asked Jeremy.

Confused, Ross screwed up his eyes, then remembered his friend's plan to escort the Fulford's back to town. "Aye, when are you leaving?"

"In ten, possibly fifteen minutes," he replied and left the breakfast room.

"Jackson! Coffee! Make it strong! And send to the stables. I want Warrior saddled and brought to the front of the house." He hoped coffee would ease his pounding head. When it arrived, he drank three cups in rapid succession.

"Perhaps you'd like this too, sir."

Ross looked at the yellowy liquid. "Good God, man! Do you intend to poison me? What is that?"

"Raw eggs and vinegar. the finest cure for a hangover known to man. Drink it in one, sir."

Eyeing him warily, Ross picked up the glass and drank the liquid. "Ugh! Disgusting! Another one of your kill or cure remedies. Bah! Awful!"

Not knowing whether Jackson's cure would ease his self-inflicted condition or make him feel worse, Ross waited in the hall for his guests to descend from their chambers. After the good wishes, the grateful thanks, and the promises to visit Lord and Lady Fulford in London, Ross bade his guests farewell.

The moment he stepped outside, the bright sunlight hit him. But determined not to succumb he mounted Warrior and alongside Jeremy, rode behind the Fulford's carriage. The servants and luggage travelled in a smaller carriage and brought up the rear.

"I've passed an agreeable time here, Ross," Jeremy said. "I'm most grateful for your hospitality and your friendship."

"None more so than I."

"And you've not forgotten your promise to stand as groomsman?"

Ross shook his head. "I won't let you down, dear friend. It will be a privilege to assist you towards the honourable state of matrimony."

Jeremy laughed. "And I'll warrant it will not be long before you join me there. We are lambs to the slaughter, dear friend. Innocently we present ourselves at the altar in the name of love."

Ross wanted to laugh with him but was out of sorts, he managed a half grin. In truth, he felt slightly envious of Jeremy because he was on his way to see his fiancée with every reason to be joyful. Silently, Ross chastised himself for begrudging his old friend true happiness.

"Who knows?" He shrugged and thrust out his hand. As ever, they parted the best of friends.

As Ross turned off the turnpike road and retraced his route back to the Grange, a couple of the admiral's farm labourers told him about the hunt for the sheep attacker. He had avoided Witton land and the route Miss Richmond rode each morning. He wasn't sure how she would greet him, or what his feelings would be when he saw her again. He had decided that it would be better if they met in company the next time he saw her.

As he rode towards Aston Hill, no matter how hard he tried, he couldn't get Miss Richmond out of his head. Last night too, her image had plagued him. He hadn't been able to sleep in his bed, despite the vast amount of brandy he had consumed. Dreams of her had come to him, constantly reminding him of his rejected proposal. He had tossed and turned, like a ship on the ocean refusing to answer her helm. When the calm had come, he had thought she was alongside him, that all had been settled between them, and she was his. Eventually he must have succumbed to some sort of slumber.

Why didn't she wish to marry? Had she been frightened by the experience of a close relative, perhaps her mother? Had his approach been too direct? Should he have given her time to warm to the idea? He knew he hadn't made his feelings clear. Jeremy had taken him to task and given him a thorough dressing down for giving up too easily. But why hadn't Miss Richmond understood? She was a sensible girl, but apparently she needed a romantic proposal from him, whether that was sensible or not.

Sensible. How he disliked the word. At sea, how many times had he opted for the *less sensible* course of action? Several times. And taking risks had paid off handsomely for him. Would bold action win fair lady? He mulled over the notion until he saw the admiral and his search party emerging from the woods.

Turning Warrior in their direction, he kicked the horse into a gallop. Then he heard it, the unmistakable discharge from a musket. The same crack he'd heard in battle, fired by French sharpshooters from their fighting tops.

The admiral's horse reared. The mare's legs gave way beneath her as she hit the ground, taking the admiral with her. Men dismounted. Calls for aid echoed down the hill. A few horses scattered, and men came running.

Quickly assessing the scene, Ross turned his mount towards the woods, determined to get the sharpshooter before he reloaded. At full gallop, he powered his way into the trees and fought through the dense undergrowth. He drove himself on, convinced the musketeer was close.

He couldn't find a twig or leaf disturbed. The wood was silent. The villain had disappeared.

Ross returned to the crowd of men and dismounted. The admiral lay flat on the ground. His mare was also down, whinnying in pain as she struggled to get to her feet.

"My horse!" The admiral bellowed. "How's the old girl?"

"Took a ball to the shoulder, sir," Walters shouted. "I'm afraid she's done for."

"Raise me up! Let me see!"

At his side, Ross had dropped to one knee. "Sir, your leg looks serious."

"I can't feel a bloody thing! Get me up! Get me up!"

Ross caught the steward's eye. "Best not move him. Where's the nearest surgeon?"

"Need to send to Portsmouth, captain." Walters looked worried, glancing at the admiral's boot as blood began to ooze out of the top.

Ross had noticed it too. "Send your best rider straightaway. Give him my horse. We'll make the admiral as comfortable as possible, but we'll not move him. We may cause him more damage by doing so. Tell your man to bring the surgeon here with all haste. And send word to Witton. Miss Richmond must be told."

"I don't want all this fuss." The admiral had begun to sweat profusely. "I'll be all right. I'm just winded...soon be on my feet."

Walters beckoned to Pride and sent him on his way. He dispatched another rider to Witton. Then he turned to where the admiral lay and knelt beside him. "Sir, the mare."

"I know," he grimaced. "Do what has to be done."

A few moments later a pistol shot rang out across the valley, scaring birds from the tree tops, followed by silence. Aware of the admiral's deteriorating condition, Ross knew there was no time to lose. He knelt at the admiral's other side. "Your leg might be broken, sir. If so, splints will be needed, but the bleeding must be staunched. We must apply a tourniquet."

The admiral nodded, and his breathing became more laboured.

"You men," Ross ordered as he pulled his stock from his neck, "hold the admiral down."

* * * *

"There's been an accident, Miss Richmond," Middleton said. "A message has arrived. The admiral's been unhorsed. They want you to come to Aston Hill—"

Bella didn't wait to hear anymore. Within moments she had ordered Merriweather saddled and changed into her riding habit. She didn't care how unladylike she appeared as she raced down the stairs and ran to the stables.

"Send a cart after me to the Witton side of Aston Hill." She kicked the mare into a gallop and took off alone. The lad who had brought the news followed with little chance of keeping up on his tired mount.

Desperately, Bella urged the mare on, determined to get to her father as soon as possible. She thought only of reaching him as she focused on her journey, urging, willing, driving Merriweather towards the scene of the accident. At full gallop, she didn't allow herself to think of what might face her when she reached her destination.

She spied the group of men half-way up the hill and galloped towards them. One of the beaters held Merriweather's bridle as she slipped from the saddle. As she approached, the crowd of men around her father parted and she saw him sprawled on the ground. Quentin looked up at her from his position kneeling at the admiral's side.

"Papa!" she cried, sinking to her knees beside him and taking his hand in hers. It was cold and clammy.

He turned his head slowly towards her. "Bella, my dear, the old girl's finally unhorsed me."

"You'll be all right." She struggled to keep her voice calm and sought Quentin's watchful eyes for confirmation of her words. There was uncertainty in his bright blue pools, possibly even hopelessness. Was he trying to tell her something? Did he know more than she had been told?

"Try to keep him conscious," Quentin whispered. "We think he's broken his leg, but there's a lot of bleeding. And he may have injured his back."

"Bella," the admiral weakly called. "I can't see you...where are you?"

"I'm here, father." She tightened her grip on his hand. "Right here. Stay with us, please."

Admiral Richmond slipped into unconsciousness.

"Father!"

* * * *

Swiftly Ross ripped open the admiral's shirt. He pressed his ear to his bare chest and breathed a sigh of relief when he heard heartbeats. He raised his head and found himself barely inches from Miss Richmond's face. So close he could feel her uneven breath on his cheek. "He's alive. We've sent for a surgeon but I don't know how long he can hang on."

"We must take him home." She pleaded, her voice filled with ragged emotion.

"No! Moving him now, before we know the true extent of his injuries, may cause…" He paused, wanting to search her eyes, but they were turned towards her father. "It wouldn't be wise."

Only inches separated them, but this was not the way he wanted things to be. Physically he felt drained, as if he had been engaged in battle. Yet, when after a fight had he been rewarded by the sight of a woman's tender face? He was close enough to touch her, the woman he had come to respect, desire, and love. Inwardly he cursed the brigand responsible for injuring an officer he had come to respect. It pained him to see a man like the admiral brought down. But more particularly, it hurt him deeply to see the woman he loved terrified that her father might slip from this world.

He had wondered how their first meeting after his proposal might be. Would he feel awkward because she had rejected him? He had resolved to bide his time, pretend he had never approached the matter. In the meantime, he would try to win her heart. But he couldn't have anticipated their present situation. He had to act decisively and give her whatever assistance she needed without reservation. Whatever happened to the admiral, one fact remained—he was in love with Bella Richmond.

Chapter Ten

The admiral arrived at Witton late in the afternoon. A room had been prepared for him under the direction of Dr. Grey, a naval surgeon from Portsmouth. Dr. Grey reported to Bella and Captain Quentin in the dining room when he had finished attending to his patient. "The admiral is settled and sleeps peacefully. I shall remain overnight with him and administer more laudanum if required."

"But the leg will mend!" Bella said, desperate for some scrap of hope that all would eventually be set to right.

Dr. Grey looked at her. "I will not give you false hope; the next few hours are crucial. I have set the bones, now he must fight any infection."

Bella paced the room, her fingers interlocked. She knew she had to be brave. Everything possible had been done for her father, thanks to the surgeon and Quentin. Her shoulders and neck ached, her limbs felt heavy, and for the first time since she had been summoned to Aston Hill, a wave of hunger surged through her stomach. Not only did it make her feel guilty, but also made her think of the others. They were guests in her establishment and she had a duty to feed them.

"It has been a long day, gentlemen, you must be famished. Please, come and eat, we have steak pie and cold ham. I have ordered a similar meal to be served in the servants' hall for all the men who helped rescue my father. Dr. Grey, I am especially indebted to you for your prompt attention and setting my father's broken bones."

"I am honoured to be of service, Miss Richmond. No naval surgeon would hesitate to come to the aid of your father at sea or on land. However, had it not been for Captain Quentin's swift action earlier today, I doubt if we could have saved him."

"Please accept my sincere gratitude, captain, and that of my father." She glanced across the table at him, barely able to look at him directly. An overwhelming desire to take his hand in hers washed over her. She swallowed deeply, grasping Quentin's hand would be most inappropriate, even if the surgeon wasn't present. But the temptation was there and she had to fight against it. She prayed he would find it in his heart to pardon her for rejecting him so bluntly the previous day, but this was not the time to beg for forgiveness.

"Like the surgeon, I'm glad to have been of service, Miss Richmond. Let's hope the admiral makes a speedy recovery."

They all nodded their agreement and settled at the table. The men ate heartily, but Bella picked at her portion. Her appetite had waned as quickly as it had gripped her. When Quentin had finished eating, he said, "There's one matter causing me concern."

Bella froze. The piece of braised steak she was about to eat remained on her plate. Surely he wasn't going to raise the question of his proposal. He couldn't possibly, not now! They had been together for most of the day, but the circumstances had been trying and not one word had passed between them relating to their previous meeting.

"Does this involve me?" The surgeon pushed his empty plate aside.

"Partially," Quentin replied. "When I approached the admiral this morning, I witnessed the single shot fired from the woods. I had assumed it came from a sharpshooter who must have been skilled with his weapon to attempt a shot at that range. The admiral was fortunate the ball missed him."

Bella gasped. "You didn't tell me this earlier! I was told it was an accident. Papa was unhorsed, and the mare had to be put down."

"Please do not distress yourself, Miss Richmond." Quentin leaned across the table towards her, and his hands moved close to hers. She retracted both of them and let them drop into her lap under the table cloth. "I do not believe this morning's incident was an accident."

"And you took it upon yourself to conceal this dastardly deed from me all day?"

Quentin looked suitably contrite. "There was little point in worrying you unduly when we didn't know the extent of your father's injuries. Concealment was not my intention, but it was imperative to clarify the facts before I related them to you. I did attempt to pursue the assailant, but to no avail."

"Tell me all the facts, please!"

"On hearing the shot, I rode into the woods. He must have been well concealed because I saw nothing of the villain. I don't know how he made his escape. However, he left a musket ball in the mare which I recovered from the carcass." He dug into his waistcoat pocket and produced the ball. Holding it between his finger and thumb, he offered it to the surgeon. "Tell me, doctor, what do you make of this?"

Dr. Grey took the item and examined it. "I've seen plenty of these before and I'll warrant you have too, Captain."

"I do not understand, gentlemen, what is the significance?" Bella asked.

"It's French, Miss Richmond," Dr. Grey replied. "You can tell from the size and the markings left by the long barrel. It's the type that Bonaparte's sharpshooters use on board ship."

"Aye, Dr. Grey, and who would use such a weapon on Admiral Richmond?"

Bella gasped, "The French tried to murder my father!"

Quentin shrugged his broad shoulders. "I don't know, but if they did, it's likely they'll try again."

"Heaven forbid!" Bella cried.

"Perhaps the admiral can shed some light on the matter when he's sufficiently recovered to discuss it." Quentin looked at the surgeon. "Have you any idea when that is likely to be?"

Dr. Grey shook his head. "I'm giving him laudanum to make him sleep. When he wakes, he'll be in pain. It could be two or three days before he'll be able to tell you anything, and even then he may not remember."

Quentin put his hand to his chin and rested his elbow on the table. "Until we know more or the villain is apprehended, you and your staff, Miss Richmond, must be vigilant."

A worried look crossed Dr. Grey's face. "It was my intention to remain until tomorrow, Miss Richmond, but I can stay longer if you require me."

"That is most considerate of you," Bella replied.

"With your permission, Miss Richmond," Quentin said, "I would also like to stay until tomorrow. I'll scout around the grounds once night has fallen and ensure a watch is posted."

Bella considered his offer for a few moments. If her father's life was in danger, she had to do whatever she could to protect him. "Thank you, captain. Your protection will be most welcome."

After they finished their meal, the men went about their respective business; Dr. Grey to his patient, and Quentin to scout the grounds. Bella changed from her riding habit into a light muslin dress and went to her small parlour to write notes to neighbours. If no news came from Witton, callers would come. She sent messengers to Penley and to the Parsonage, and considered writing to her cousin in London, but quickly dismissed the idea. Her father had told him not to visit. Besides, the thought of seeing him again, regardless of the circumstances, was abhorrent to her. Perhaps she was neglecting her family duty by excluding Mr. Richmond but to give the odious man the opportunity to place himself legitimately under their roof was intolerable.

Her note writing complete, she sat for a few hours with her father. When Dr. Grey came to relieve her, she returned to the small parlour to sit alone for a while. But the room was uncomfortably hot. The back of her neck felt damp as she touched the base of her hairline with her fingers. Anxious to get some air into the room, she pushed up the tall sash window and sat on the cushioned seat next to the sill. It was one of her favourite places in the house, where she could be completely alone with her thoughts and, occasionally, her dreams.

What a catastrophic day it had been. Seeing her dearly beloved father hovering on the edge of life, not knowing if his next breath would be his last, had taken its toll on her. She felt weary, her eyelids were heavy, but she couldn't contemplate placing her head on a pillow. Her senses were far too raw and her feelings in turmoil.

She gazed at the sky from the open window. It was one of those summer evenings when the sun casts a wonderful red glow in the heavens. Only a few strips of cloud dared to blot an otherwise perfect, magenta sky. A few stars came out and as they began to sparkle, her thoughts drifted to Quentin.

Calm, capable, and in command of the situation, he had behaved impeccably, with no hint that their previous parting had been less than cordial. His strength had supported her through those difficult moments when her father lay wounded on the ground. Thinking of the hours they waited for the surgeon made her realised how much she admired him, not only for his physical attractiveness but also for his strong character. And as she dwelt further on her admiration for him, she realised she had probably been in his company more today than at any other time during their acquaintance.

Quentin had probably saved the admiral's life by applying the correct pressure to his injured limb. As he had knelt with her at her father's side, she had felt his warm breath on her face. Occasionally, she had caught the way he looked at her and seen pain in his eyes. Shame that her rejection of his proposal might have been responsible for some of that pain made her feel very small inside.

"What are you doing sitting next to an open window with the light behind you?" Quentin demanded from outside.

Startled, she glared at him. "How long have you been hiding there?"

"Only a few moments—but it was more than long enough for an assassin to have taken your life."

"Oh, damnation, why am I so foolish?" She jumped down from the window seat, retreated into the room, and snuffed out the candles. Moonlight continued to stream in as she watched Quentin's tall figure step over the sill and enter the house.

With one deft action, he closed the bottom half of the sash and fixed the window on its latch. Turning, he advanced towards her. "An elegant choice of words, although somewhat unexpected."

"What are you doing in here?"

"I believe I'm following my instincts."

Her fingers began to tingle. She took a deep breath and her breasts pressed against the confining bodice of her dress. "Is someone trying to murder me too?"

"They'll answer to me if they are."

With his broad shoulders squared against the window, it was too dark to see the expression on his face. But she took comfort in the strength of his presence. A warm sensation flickered to life in the pit of her stomach, welled up, and caught in her throat. She swallowed deeply.

"Are you afraid of me?" He stepped closer.

"Why should I be?" Aware of her body heat rising, she ran her tongue over her lips to moisten them.

For several moments, she stood facing him in silence. What was passing between them? She struggled to understand the meaning of the moment until his warm hands touched her upper arms, flesh on flesh. Unable to resist, she allowed herself to be drawn to him, as if a hidden power radiated from his masculine torso. Excitement coursed through her as the warmth of his body pervaded hers.

As he lowered his head, she sensed his soft breath close by. Her hands came up to his chest and rested close to his neck, as his arms enveloped her. She pressed herself against him, tilted her head up to his, closed her eyes, and felt his lips touch hers. His kiss, tentative at first, gently drew her closer as her need for him grew. This was so new; she had never been kissed like this before. With his mouth upon hers, soft and pliant, passion flared between them.

Her light muslin gown, once cool for the humid evening, clung to her. Sensations beyond her wildest dreams raced through her as he held her firmly. The touch of his lips on hers sent her inner emotions into chaotic confusion. Time stood still between them as she embraced him. Her fingers slid to the back of his neck and caressed the soft down at the base of his hairline.

When he finally released her, Bella's legs had weakened. The sensations he had created within her were like nothing she had known before. He stood facing her for several moments in the moonlight. She looked up at him and, unable to tear her gaze away, struggled to understand what had passed between them.

He stepped back. "Forgive me, I had no right to kiss you."

She wanted to open her heart to him, but too much had happened that day. Confused, she struggled to speak sensibly. "Why…why did you kiss me?"

"I saw you standing in the moonlight and the temptation was too great."

Her heart leapt and her hopes soared. She had never felt anything so wonderful before. But the sensible part of Bella Richmond re-emerged from temporary slumber. A lady should not stand in the moonlight with a man to whom she was not engaged and allow him to kiss her. And that lady should not be kissing him back.

"Forgive me, Captain Quentin. This should not have happened." In full retreat, she ran through the open door.

* * * *

Bella needed the sanctuary of her bedchamber, to be alone with her thoughts, and to reconcile her feelings. But she couldn't pass the sickroom without checking on her father's progress. A room had been hurriedly made up for him on the ground floor of Witton. She stood in the doorway, settling her emotions before she entered.

During the long day on Aston Hill, she had watched him drift in and out of consciousness. Worried his next breath may be his last she had held his hand and urged him to fight against his pain.

"Laudanum will help him while I set his bones," Dr. Grey had said. "The admiral may have damaged his back. I cannot say for sure, but I recommend he is strapped to a board and laid flat. Only then can he be safely transported home. He must continue to be kept on his back until the extent of his injury is known."

Bella had admired the surgeon's skill as she had watched him remove the makeshift tourniquet and staunch the blood flow. He had cleaned her father's wound and straightened his bones. The injured limb had been splinted. Her father's life had been saved.

Dr. Grey stood up as she entered the room.

"How is he?" Bella asked.

"The admiral is sleeping, but when he wakes the pain will be severe. Do you wish to sit with him for a while?"

"Yes."

He walked towards the door. "I will be outside if you need me."

In silence, she took comfort in the gentle rise and fall of his chest. But it was agony to see him incapacitated, and she worried about how long it would take for him to recover. Aged fifty-six, he might suffer a long period of invalidity. However, he was alive, and she knew she ought to be grateful for that.

Her muscles tightened in her neck and shoulders; she felt guilty about her feelings for Quentin. Throughout the turmoil of the day, they had been so close. She had tried over and over again to push all thoughts of him to the back of her mind. Her attempts had been futile. Her feelings, so recently aroused, refused to be quelled.

In the dim candlelight in the sickroom, she lost herself and relived those few precious moments when she had discovered the strength of a man's arms around her. The memory of his touch and the masculine smell of leather and sandalwood returned to her vividly. The passion she had felt in their kiss carried her as if upon a huge wave. How could one kiss have been so powerful and yet so sweet?

She shook her head, determined to put him out of her thoughts. But how could she? He had kissed her, and she had kissed him back. And she had told him that she had no intention of marrying? Oh, those foolish, silly words!

If only she could turn the clock back, live those moments again, and respond to him as she had done tonight. Was all lost? Couldn't she explain that she had reacted hastily to his proposal? And if he felt inclined to renew his advances, she would be happy to accept.

Was she ready to be a wife? Oh, how she longed to say yes, but how could she? Her father needed her, but for how long? Would he make a complete recovery? As mistress of his house, she had to continue in that role, whatever her feelings for Quentin might be. Her duty lay with her father.

The stress of the day hung heavily upon her. Two large tears rolled down her cheeks. Hastily she wiped them away as she heard Dr. Grey's footsteps approaching.

* * * *

Bella spent a fitful night, tossing and turning in her bed. Images of Quentin, her father, and the dark eyes of the highwayman who had abducted her all became wrapped up in a nightmare. One moment in her dreams she had been captured, the next Quentin rescued her, and finally her father welcomed her with open arms. But one face would not leave her—Quentin's. Dozing she relived the touch of his lips and kissed her pillow. She woke, determined to speak to him as soon as possible.

"Captain Quentin left early for Portsmouth," Middleton said. "He's gone to report yesterday's incident to the magistrates. He's also brought some of his own men from the Grange to stand guard around the estate."

The butler's news didn't surprise her. As a natural leader, Quentin would hardly wait around to be told what to do. He would do his duty as he saw fit. She felt the same; her duty lay with her father, but it didn't stop her thinking about the captain astride his hunter on the Portsmouth Road.

Dr. Grey stood up when Bella entered the sickroom. She glanced at him and thought she saw a deep concern in his face. "How is my father?"

"The admiral continues to sleep off the laudanum," he replied.

"Has he woken at all?"

"No, Miss Richmond, but when he does wake, I expect him to be in pain. I'll remain until then and decide on the next course of treatment when I can assess his condition."

"Thank you. I will sit with him for a few hours."

"I'm grateful for the chance to sleep." He turned to leave. "Please, Miss Richmond, do not hesitate to have me woken if the admiral takes a turn for the worse."

Bella nodded, knowing her father had a long road to recovery ahead of him. Quietly she took up her post at his bedside and tried to think of her father in happier times, but she couldn't stop her thoughts drifting to Captain Ross Quentin.

* * * *

By mid-morning callers started to arrive at Witton. Some neighbours came in person while others sent notes with a servant. Middleton dealt with most of the enquiries. However, when he stepped into the sickroom to tell her Reverend Winters had arrived, Bella felt obliged to receive the parson herself.

"Mr. Winters is accompanied by his wife, Miss. They are waiting in the drawing room."

Bella stood up and straightened the front of her gown. She had sent a note to the parsonage, so Mr. Winters was expected, but Mrs. Winters too! Her heart sank; it would take all her self-control to be civil to the parson's wife. She pressed her lips together, took a deep breath, and remembered her duty as mistress of the house. Leaving the sickroom to the admiral's valet, she went to greet them.

After Bella invited them to sit down, Mr. Winters enquired about the admiral's health. Unusually, Mrs. Winters remained silent. They listened intently to Bella's account of the incident.

When she had finished, Mr. Winters sprang to his feet and started to wring his hands. "What dreadful news! What next? Will we all be murdered in our beds? Is the whole country overrun with thieves and vagabonds?"

"I do not know the answers to your questions, Mr. Winters," Bella replied. "Neither do we know who was responsible for attempting to shoot my father, but Captain Quentin and his men are investigating."

"Good, I am relieved that something is being done." He glanced at his wife and added, "We have been praying for the admiral's speedy recovery."

"Thank you." Bella looked quickly from one to the other and hoped they would soon be gone.

Mrs. Winters fussed over her gown as she sat on the sofa. "It must be a great comfort to have the love and support of your cousin. I assume you will delay the announcement of your engagement for a few weeks, until the admiral's health is restored."

Weary from lack of sleep and worry over her father, Bella could hardly believe what she was hearing. She bit her lower lip, determined not to let her annoyance get the better of her. After all, it wasn't Mrs. Winters fault she had been misinformed. Bella decided to set her right. "Mrs. Winters, you have been misinformed. I am not engaged to my cousin, Mr. Richmond. I never have been, and I never will be."

Mrs. Winters jaw dropped. It took her a few seconds to reply. "But we had it from the gentleman himself. He spoke to us only the day before yesterday."

"I repeat, you have been misinformed. And if a certain gentleman has been broadcasting false information about me throughout the neighbourhood, I can only conclude that he is no gentleman."

"Oh! My goodness, I have been drawn into a web of deceit. My most humble apologies, Miss Richmond. It was not my intention to spread false rumour. You must understand, I thought the arrangement rather unusual. He rarely visits, and I know you have not been in town these past few years."

"I am sure, Mr. and Mrs. Winters, now you are fully aware of the correct intelligence you will both be most diligent in quelling any ill-informed rumour-mongering."

"Of course, you may rely upon us. But if you would excuse me, I believe my place is at the admiral's side, where I can offer a few prayers for his speedy recovery." Mr. Winters turned on his heel and left the room.

Mrs. Winters shifted nervously on the sofa. "I do hope you will not hold this unfortunate business about your cousin against me, Miss Richmond. For I greatly value your acquaintance and would be most miserable should I find that you would not see me again."

For the first time since her father's injury a small smile came to Bella's lips. "You were mislead, Mrs.

Winters, by my inscrutable cousin. I am ashamed to call him a relative of mine, but I cannot deny the connection. Please accept my apologies on his behalf, for he is no longer welcome in this house. Be assured, you have not offended me and remain welcome."

"Oh, thank you, Miss Richmond. I shall do everything in my power to right this dreadful misunderstanding."

Their conversation was cut short when Middleton entered. "Mr. Cope is waiting in the hall, Miss Richmond."

"Excuse me, Mrs. Winters, but I must speak to him urgently. Middleton, show him to the library." Bella stood up, "Thank you so much for calling, Mrs. Winters. Please remain seated and wait here for your husband."

In the library Bella found her father's solicitor. "I trust you have not been kept waiting, Mr. Cope."

"Not at all, Miss Richmond. I hope you do not think this in an intrusion, but upon receipt of your note at my office, I thought it prudent to call. The admiral may be in need of my professional services."

＊＊＊＊

Ross ached in every limb. He'd ridden to Portsmouth and back and trawled the local inns for information. A bank of misty fog moved along the valley, turning the weather to drizzle. He reined in, pulled his boat cloak out of his saddle pack, and wrapped it around his shoulders.

The pounding of approaching horses put him on his guard. All day, he had been gathering intelligence, and from the information he had received he had learned to be cautious. The magistrate had related cases of highway robbery in the area, and several young girls, mostly servants, had been abducted. The accounts were too similar to Miss Richmond's experience to not be connected. Also, the innkeepers he had spoken with would quickly spread the news that a man of his description was on the lookout for anyone carrying a French long musket. He reached for his sidearm and took cover in the nearby trees.

Three riders came along the road going south. They wore box capes with collars raised and tri-cornered hats pulled well down. He couldn't make out their faces as they rode by; however, he noticed that one carried a French style musket on his back.

Initially tempted to follow them, Ross held back. The weapon's similarity to the one fired at the admiral might be coincidental. Also, daylight was fading. He could trail them all night only to find they were collecting a coach for their master. He waited until they were out of sight before he emerged and rejoined the road homewards.

* * * *

The next morning Ross made an early start. Anxious for news of the admiral, he rode towards Witton land. Despite yesterday's rainfall, the cool morning air proved pleasantly refreshing. Exhausted by his ride and the tension accrued from the shooting incident, he had slept well the previous night. Not even Miss Richmond's image had disturbed him.

However, today she was back on his mind. He couldn't forget holding her in his arms. The sensations she had awakened in him had sent his reason spiralling out of control. He yearned to press her to his chest and taste the soft suppleness of her lips again.

He marvelled at those unexpected moments when his memory brought forth tantalizing images of her. How soft her lips had felt against his. Light and gentle at first, then building crescendo-like until the sensation had erupted through his body. During their brief encounter in the moonlight, he hadn't been able to stop himself kissing her, and he would have kissed her again, if she hadn't backed away.

He kicked his horse into a gallop, determined to master his feelings for her. He approached the gatekeeper's cottage and eased Warrior to a walk before reining in. A heavy chain secured the gates.

Jackson emerged from his lookout post and touched his cap. "Good morning, Captain." He turned the key in the padlock and opened one of the large iron gates.

"All's well?"

"Yes, Captain. Neighbours came and went yesterday. I shouldn't think Miss Richmond had a minute's peace. The reverend and his lady went home, but Lady Mary stayed the night. She sent her manservant for her things, and he brought her maid."

"Any news of the admiral?"

"Last I heard he was 'comfortable,' whatever that's supposed to mean. Comfortable recovering or comfortable on his death bed, eh?"

"Jackson, you're a pessimistic moaner. Will you ever change?"

"Why should I? Expect the worst and then what comes is usually better." He shut the gate with a loud clang.

As the driveway stretched out before him, Ross nudged Warrior into a trot. His heart pounded on every rise in the saddle, as each stride brought him closer to Miss Richmond.

He checked himself as he dismounted, realising he would need all his self-discipline to control his feelings. He couldn't allow himself to be alone with her. The temptation was too great. Not only did he want to embrace her, but he also wanted to savour the sweetness of her kisses. He took a deep breath and tried to close his mind to her image and the feelings her picture evoked. But in his heart he knew he wanted to marry Miss Richmond more than ever.

Chapter Eleven

When Ross arrived at Witton, Middleton announced him to the ladies in the breakfast room.

"Won't you join us?" Miss Richmond gestured to a seat opposite Lady Mary.

Ross sat down. "Thank you, Miss Richmond, but I have already breakfasted. What news of the admiral?"

Miss Richmond smiled. "He is awake. But I had to leave him to his valet when Dr. Grey said he wanted to change the dressings. The leg will remain in splints until the bones have healed, of course. But judging by my father's gruff dismissal of me this morning, I am confident he is on the mend."

"Good news indeed," agreed Ross, who tried to concentrate on Lady Mary but found he couldn't stop looking at Miss Richmond. It pleased him greatly to see her in better spirits than she had been the day before.

Lady Mary dabbed her mouth with her napkin. "Are you any nearer to apprehending the villain?"

"No, my lady. I've unearthed a few clues and numerous reports of suspicious characters roaming the countryside. However, nothing linked to the shooting incident." He had decided not to tell them about the three riders he had seen on the road.

"Miss Richmond had implied that the shot may have been of French origin."

"Yes, my lady, but it proves little. Since the peace, many have returned to England with souvenirs from French and Spanish campaigns. Without positive proof to link a man to the scene, we may never find the perpetrators."

Miss Richmond's teaspoon slipped out of her hand and clattered on the table. "You believe there was more than one man involved?"

"Possibly, but I cannot be sure. The sharpshooter may have been a hired henchman. If so, who would want to take the admiral's life?" He paused, believing his question might have been too insensitive.

"Only myself and the trustees my father has appointed to manage my inheritance." Miss Richmond said.

"Is your cousin a trustee?"

Miss Richmond shook her head. "Mr. Richmond would gain nothing. The estate isn't entailed. When he left a few days ago, we didn't part on the best of terms. But I fail to see how he could prosper from my father's passing."

They curtailed their conversation when Dr. Grey entered the room. He hovered at one end of the table. "Miss Richmond, it is time for me to return to Portsmouth. I have done all I can. The admiral's recovery now depends upon his care in the sickroom. Clean dressings must be applied regularly. Laudanum may be administered but only when he can't sleep. And, Miss Richmond, try to ensure that your father doesn't have any brandy."

Cheered by the surgeon's news, Ross couldn't help smiling to himself at the suggestion that the admiral might consume too much liquor. "May I sit with him for the rest of the morning?"

"Of course, Captain Quentin," Miss Richmond replied.

As he rose to leave, he couldn't help looking at her and admiring her calmness. She had endured hours of uncertainty over her father's survival. The admiral had recovered consciousness, but the battle for his health was far from won.

* * * *

When the door had closed behind Quentin, Lady Mary turned back to Bella. "I am much relieved to hear better news of your father. If it is agreeable to you, can I take the afternoon watch?"

"Indeed and thank you, Mary, it's good to have the support of loyal friends in times of need." She looked at the mantel clock as it struck. "Time is moving on, and I have much to do. There's a large volume of correspondence requiring my attention, and I must speak to cook."

"Perhaps I could assist with your letters?"

"Your help would be welcome indeed. Our neighbours have expressed their concern in their notes. I'm sure they wouldn't mind receiving a reply from you. I have the correspondence, along with pen and paper, in the morning room."

Arm in arm, they went into the next room. Bella settled her friend at the escritoire. She supplied Lady Mary with a pile of notes and writing materials, before leaving for the kitchen.

When Bella returned half an hour later, Lady Mary had finished the last note. She glanced up at her young friend. "Have you been able to speak privately to Captain Quentin?"

From her tone Bella understood the exact meaning behind her friend's question. "No, not yet." Her voice was but a half-whisper.

Lady Mary placed the pen in the holder on the writing slope. "Has it been too difficult?"

"No," Bella answered quickly, thinking of the evening he had kissed her. Or had she kissed him? She began to pace the room. "Before, I had no intention of marrying because I was comfortable and content being mistress of my father's house. I didn't think I would ever feel differently. Until now." She stopped pacing and sank onto the settee near the window. "I must take care of my father, as any dutiful daughter would. So even if I did wish to marry, how could I leave Papa?"

Lady Mary stood up, crossed the room, and sat by her friend. She placed her hand over Bella's. "It's too soon. You're confused. Falling in love seems simple at first, but often the path to true love is not made easy. You have to come to terms with your feelings. You don't know whether to jump for joy or pine for the next moment you can see him. It's foolish, isn't it, the way we feel?"

Bella sighed. "How fortunate I am to have a friend who understands me so well."

Lady Mary squeezed Bella's hand. "Of course, you must look to your father. No one, not even Captain Quentin, would expect you to do otherwise. He would be the first person to understand the importance of doing one's duty. But do not close your heart to him, for I am convinced he truly loves you, and he'll be prepared to wait."

Bella took comfort in her friend's words. She knew she needed time to come to terms with the feelings Quentin stirred within her, to allow her father to recover, and most of all, to adjust to the idea of becoming a wife. But one anxiety plagued her heart. How long could he wait? If the peace treaty was broken, she knew he would go back to sea.

* * * *

The man Ross saw in the sickroom was a very pale shadow of the robust gentleman he had come to like. Under Dr. Grey's instruction, the admiral lay flat on his back and had to remain so until the severe bruising healed. The broken leg, splinted and heavily bandage, rested on several pillows. Bedridden and confined to a recumbent position, Ross imagined the admiral had difficulty eating and drinking.

"Who's that?"

"Quentin, sir."

"Where are you? Come to my side where I can see you."

Ross moved closer.

"I'm glad that you've come. I understand I've got you to thank. You saved the leg and stopped me bleeding to death. I'm obliged to you."

"I'm not here for thanks, sir." Ross placed a chair at the side of the bed and sat down.

"I'm damn glad to see you. At last I can get an accurate report of what happened. The truth, mind. I've had enough genteel explanation from the ladies, and that surgeon's not much better. He says I'm not to ask questions. Fiddlesticks! Tell me, exactly what happened!"

Ross explained all he knew of the incident and what he had discovered since. But the admiral drifted in and out of sleep. When he woke, often with a start, he needed reassurance about his injury. However, Ross found he had to explain what had happened on Aston Hill more than once. He put the admiral's anxiety and repeated requests down to the effects of the powerful pain killer the surgeon had administered. He had seen its effects on men before and knew that laudanum might take several days to clear the admiral's system. It could take even longer if he were given more.

When Lady Mary came to relieve him at noon, Ross was more than ready to leave the sickroom. Although he had volunteered, the watch reminded him too much of calls upon wounded men after battle. Visiting the injured was a commander's duty, which he would never have shirked, but he took no pleasure in the responsibility.

In the long silent moments when the admiral had drifted off to sleep, Ross had thought of Miss Richmond. He had struggled all morning to keep her out of his mind, and failed. So, when Lady Mary arrived to take the next watch, he decided to return to the Grange.

Middleton hovered in the hall as he left the sickroom. "Do you return directly to Aston Grange, sir?" He asked as he handed Ross's hat, gloves, and riding crop to him.

"Yes, I can do no more here today. I shall return to visit the admiral tomorrow. Please tell Miss Richmond."

* * * *

Bella received Quentin's message in the morning room. Disappointed that he hadn't come to take his leave in person, she rushed to the window. She caught sight of him on the far side of the garden, making his way to the stables. Picking up her skirts, she ran after him. She reached him just as Pride led Warrior into the yard.

"Forgive me chasing after you in this manner," she panted, "but I must speak to you before you leave."

"Are you quite well?" He asked, looking at her intently.

"I'm quite well, although a little tired perhaps." She realized her behaviour was drawing attention from Pride and his stable lads. Not wishing to be overheard, she moved towards the stables. "Can we go inside?"

Quentin nodded. She led him into an empty stall, the one where the admiral's mare used to be kept, and turned to face him. "Forgive me, I couldn't let you go without some explanation."

He removed his hat and smiled at her, briefly exposing his near perfect teeth. Standing with his feet apart he looked at her expectantly. "What is so urgent?"

Bella took a deep breath "I was rather hasty when I told you I had no intention of marrying. I was in error. What I meant is after my London Season, I had decided not to marry, but when I made your acquaintance…"

She stopped, unsure of how to continue, for he had closed the distance between them. Her shoulders tensed. She thought he intended to kiss her and she knew she shouldn't have been there in the stable with him. As she looked up at him, she felt his warm breath on her face and her eyes locked with his.

"By all the seas, Miss Richmond, are you telling me you've changed your mind?"

How could she answer him? Yesterday she would have welcomed his suit. But now, her duty as a daughter took precedence. "Please I don't think you understand. If could marry, I would. There's no other for me."

"Nor for me." Then, as if what she had been trying to say registered with him, he stepped back. "What do you mean, if you could marry? Why can't you marry?"

"My father needs me."

"You can't sacrifice your happiness for an ageing parent!"

"He needs me now!"

"And I need you too, Miss Richmond, more than any woman I've ever known. There must be some way we can resolve this. I could make Witton my home if that's what you want, as long as I can be with you."

"Even if we lived at Witton, what will happen when you go back to sea?" Her hand flew to her mouth, as if to hide the words she had just spoken, but it was too late. The real question had been asked.

He took another step back. "This is nothing to do with your father, is it?"

The tension spread from her shoulders along the length of her spine. She couldn't move, she couldn't speak, she could barely breathe.

"You're terrified of being left alone, aren't you? Is it something to do with your mother? Did she detest the months, or was it years, she had to wait alone for her husband's return?"

Bella stiffened, as if a huge spring inside her was winding up tighter and tighter. He had discovered her secret fear. And the ease with which he had been able to uncover her vulnerability shook her to her very core. An only child, she had constantly been at her mother's side throughout her formative years. She had been loved, indulged, and pampered, while her mother had grieved silently for her absent husband. Now years later, with her inner fear exposed, helplessness swept over her and left her drained of emotion.

Quentin looked into her eyes. "You may be content to bury what's between us somewhere deep in your memory, but I'm not. I want you to be my wife. I can't promise I will never return to the sea. As an admiral's daughter, you know you cannot expect a sailor to make such a vow. My feelings for you, Miss Richmond are genuine, but do not ask me to choose between you and the sea. My love for both is inseparable. I asked you to share my life because I thought you understood me. I am but an honest sailor with salt in his veins and true love in his heart."

Bella felt as if she was clinging to a rock in a violent storm. Her heart pounded fiercely, her blood pulsated along her veins, and for a few dizzy moments, she almost forgot to breathe.

"This is not the time or place to discuss our future." He took a few paces towards the stable doors. "I will leave you to tend to your father."

Stunned, Bella stood in the shadow of the fallen mare's stable. It took her several moments to recover her senses. When she reached the stable door, she was just in time to watch him ride away.

* * * *

Lady Mary remained at Witton and regularly kept company with the admiral during the following week. On several occasions Bella wanted to confess to her friend what had happened in the stable, but she held back at the last moment. She examined her feelings and found the fear of long separation would not leave her. Although Quentin had offered to live under the admiral's roof, could that really be a solution? For Quentin and the admiral, but not for her. She would still have to endure life apart from her husband when he went to sea. In her lowest moments a flicker of hope still kindled within her, like the last embers in the ashes. All was not lost. Lady Mary hadn't stayed at home. She had sailed with her beloved Charles over miles of ocean.

But Quentin said he wouldn't have wives of officers on board. His very words echoed like the solemn clang of a tenor bell, reminding her that moments of marital bliss could be followed by anxious years waiting for news. Would she be like her mother? Would she fade in Quentin's absence? She recalled the day her father had returned and found his wife gone. There was only her gravestone to mourn over. If she married Quentin, would their fate be similar?

She dreamed of him each night, and he was in her thoughts when she woke in the morning. But why was he avoiding her? He had called daily at Witton throughout the week. But during his visits to the admiral, she had never been alone with him. Did he no longer trust himself with her?

When household duties were complete, her thoughts returned to those few stolen moments in the stable and his final words: "I am but an honest sailor with salt in his veins and true love in his heart."

* * * *

At Dr. Grey's insistence, the admiral remained flat on his back. A bed had been set up for him with a board placed over the mattress. The admiral complained bitterly about the arrangement. His room was small and located on the side of the house with neither a view of the garden, nor the drive. He disliked being confined there and often moaned to Bella about it. When she wasn't there, he ordered the servants to bring him books and newspapers from the library.

As Bella came into the sickroom, the admiral called to her. "Come and look in the *London Gazette*, there's an announcement from Quentin."

Her heart skipped a beat as she thought of the captain. She picked up the newspaper and fingered the pages. "Where is it?"

"With the announcements!"

She glared at him. "A week of bed-rest has restored the volume of your voice, Papa. Let us hope your leg mends as quickly."

"What else can I do other than lie here and roar? Can't you find it? It's about Quentin's father, Colonel Quentin."

Bella glanced quickly over the columns, then at her father. "No, I can't. What about the colonel?"

"He's got a new son! Good to know there's life in the old dog yet, eh?" The admiral chuckled. "I was talking about the old fellow to Quentin a few days ago. Do you know, Bella, he's a year older than me?"

"No, Papa, I didn't."

"He's got a young wife, of course. She's not much older than the captain. A handsome lady too, by all accounts. A widow you know. No children of her own, until now, of course. She's very similar to Lady Mary, though not titled. And to think," he laughed loudly "only a year after the wedding! Puts some of the young bucks to shame, eh?"

"Indeed, sir."

"Bella, something's troubling me. I've been meaning to discuss it with you. Come alongside." When she had settled herself on the edge of his bed, he took her hand. "I've had plenty of time to think, laid up like this. About my trustees; the two I've named are old men. It was fine when I was at sea, since I knew they'd look after you and your mother. But when something like this happens to a fellow, it makes him think seriously about the future."

"You're on the road to recovery, Papa. Dr. Grey says—"

"Yes, he says a lot except how long I'm to be laid up here. I want to get out of this room and go back to my comfortable bed. I know a broken leg doesn't mend in a few weeks, but there's nothing wrong with my back. I'm tired of being strapped to this board."

"You must be patient, father."

"Bah! Patience never got me anything worth having. Back to my trustees; now what about your cousin Granville?"

"Father!" Bella jumped to her feet. "Has your fall addled your brain?"

"No, dear," he chuckled. "I wanted to tease you a little. But seeing a frown on your brow, I'm sorry. Come back here." He patted the side of his bed where she had been sitting.

She resumed her seat. "I hoped we'd heard the last of him."

"I'd never consider him. His reputation got blackened in my copy book after his audacious behaviour on our very doorstep. Do not fear; I shall have nothing more to do with the fellow."

"In that we are of one mind, Papa. The less I hear of my cousin, the better."

"Your mother had a few cousins, but I've not heard of them in years. I'd not be content to leave your interests in the hands of strangers." He paused for a few moments, his face creasing as if in serious thought. "Of course, it would be different if you were married."

Bella felt her cheeks start to pink. Had Quentin said anything to him? "You know how I feel about marriage."

"You're still young and very pretty, my dear. Is there a gentleman who might take your fancy?"

Bella knew he was trying to draw her into saying something about Quentin. She decided to be equally vague. "Possibly, but one has to be careful, there are some gentlemen who are only interested in your estate."

"Oh, we're back to Granville again, are we?"

"No, Papa, but you know perfectly well there's no shortage of suitors when there's a fortune to be had."

"Yes, Lady Mary said more or less the same thing the other day."

"And what else has she been saying while sitting at your bedside?"

"She thinks we should look for a suitable husband for you. She says that with the peace there are plenty of choices. She suggested another London Season, or perhaps a few weeks in Bath."

"Did she indeed?" Bella raised her eyebrows, determined to make light of her ladyship's proposals. "How about placing an advertisement in the *Naval Chronicle*? Let me see. 'Admiral's daughter would like husband in all haste to placate ageing father.'"

He roared until his laughter turned to cries of pain. "Ah, my leg hurts! See what you've made me do!" When he had calmed down, he said, "You could do worse than marry a navy man."

Bella's pinked cheeks flamed to crimson. "Perhaps, but I believe you are biased."

"That as might be, but I am rational. What about young Quentin? He did ask my permission to speak to you. I don't suppose he's raised the subject, has he?"

Stubbornly Bella didn't answer. She didn't want to lie to her father. She couldn't. But she didn't want to go into a long explanation of why she had initially turned him down. Silence was her only resort.

"He's the pick of the fleet. You could do much worse. Of course, like most men, he'll probably need a bit of encouragement. But I don't think a man like him will be around for much longer. According to Lady Mary, he's the catch of the Season. I'm told he'll get snapped up pretty quickly. It wouldn't surprise me if the poor fellow's hounded from pillar to post by women throwing themselves at his feet—"

"Father, I believe you've made your point."

Grasping her hand, he drew her close. "I only want your happiness, my dear. I like the fellow. You know I'd be prodigiously proud to call him my son-in-law."

"And I'm sure Captain Quentin would be honoured to be part of our family," she said softly, so softly that she doubted if he heard her.

"Yes, I'm convinced of it. He'd be an excellent choice. But it's my long held belief that the prospect of successful matrimony rests with the parties concerned. It is not my affair, but time weighs heavy with me at present. I am laid up here, with little to amuse my curious mind." He started to scratch his jaw. Then, as if inspired, he said, "What if I marry again? If old Colonel Quentin can father a son, perhaps there's hope for me, eh?"

Bella didn't know what to say. Was he being serious or joking? Then she recalled how friendly he had become of late with Lady Mary. Was he thinking of her? But would she consider marriage again after her beloved Charles? "You must do whatever you consider to be appropriate, Papa."

Chapter Twelve

Bella rose early and opened her bedchamber window. Exhilarated by the morning air, she felt ready to face anything. Yesterday's clouds had cleared. The warm sun was rapidly drying out the ground. It would be perfect for riding, she decided.

Ensuring that her father was in good spirit, she left him with his valet, but did not mention where she was going, or of her intention to ride. Had he known, he might have forbidden her excursion. When she reached the stables, dressed in her riding habit, Pride looked uneasy.

"I must ride to the Grange."

"Begging pardon, Miss, but can't I or one of the lads go for you?"

"No, I have urgent business with Captain Quentin."

Reluctantly, he had Merriweather brought out and helped his mistress into the saddle. Mounted on a sturdy cob, he followed dutifully in her wake.

With her mare at a comfortable trot, Bella relished the freedom riding gave her. She breathed in deeply as she took in the beauty of the parkland surrounding her home. How long would it be hers?

Yesterday, when her father joked about remarrying, she had realized he had no notion of how her mother had missed him during the long periods of separation. His wife's decline had been hidden from him while he was away at sea. He saw only her joyful face at his home-coming and thought she was content with her life. The admiral had not experienced his wife's low moods or lived through the months of her demise in the sickroom. If she chose a similar life with Quentin, what would be her lot?

The thought of isolation plagued her. Or was it change that she disliked? She could remain in her father's house. Quentin would certainly agree to that, at least, for when he was at sea. But what would happen if her father remarried? The role of mistress of Witton would automatically go to his new wife.

Thinking for a few moments, she recalled her conversation with Quentin about parents finding happiness in old age. As she thought more of her father, the idea of him finding a wifely companion began to grow on her. If her father remarried, she would be free to marry Quentin. She kicked Merriweather to a gallop and left Pride some distance behind.

The overwhelming feelings she felt for Quentin burgeoned by the hour. Each private moment, she yearned for his arms. When she closed her eyes, she relived his soft sublime kiss. When she held her breath, she swore she felt his lips on hers. How foolish she would be to fight against her love for him any longer.

When she reached the Grange, Sanders greeted her. "I'm afraid the captain left at first light with a working party. They're cutting a drainage ditch at the long meadow, between the turnpike road and Aston Hill." He turned toward a second rider trotting towards them.

"My groom," she said. "I was in rather a hurry."

"Is it essential that you see the captain, Miss? Would you like to leave a message? I'll see that he gets it with all haste."

"No message, other than I have called. I'll return to the Witton via Aston Hill. Perhaps I'll find him there myself. Thank you, Sanders."

"It's a pleasure, Miss Richmond."

With Pride's assistance, Bella remounted and together they took the main coaching road from Portsmouth. As they cantered north along the turnpike road, they passed a small coach and four going in the opposite direction. Handled by a driver, the coach also carried an out-rider, who sported a long musket on his back. Bella thought there was a passenger, but couldn't be certain. No one acknowledged her as she passed.

As she approached Aston Hill, she recalled the attempt on her father's life on the far side. For the first time that morning, a shiver of fear crept down her spine. She signalled to Pride and reined in. "Can you see the work party?"

"Yes, Miss, over yonder in the long meadow."

Walking their horses, they approached the excavation site. As they drew nearer, Bella saw some men were up to their waists in the muddy water. Wooden stakes had been driven into the mud. A large timber A-frame, with thick ropes attached to it, supported the wooden posts, while another served as a pile-driver.

As she leaned forwards and patted Merriweather, she saw Quentin. Her heart skipped a beat. Knee deep in water, he stood with his dark hair sleeked back. His broad shoulders were bare, and his pantaloons wet through.

He turned and, without taking his eyes off her, strode towards her.

Her mouth went dry as she noticed how the sun glistened on the honed male muscle of his torso. He pulled his kerchief from his neck, wiped his face with it, and dried his hands. Soaked with water, his buckskins clung to his narrow hips, outlining his muscular thighs.

"Miss Richmond," he called and waved to one of the men to throw him a shirt, "to what do I owe the pleasure of your company? Is the admiral—?"

"He's fine," she squeaked and then realized she needed to drop her voice at least an octave. "Can I have a word with you?"

His lips quivered slightly, but she couldn't make out if he was amused or annoyed. He shook out the shirt and pushed his head and arms into it. The thin cotton fabric clung to his wet torso. His dark chest hair, exposed at the open neck, lay moist and flat.

Blushing, she tried to conceal her embarrassment behind a cough. Convinced that every eye was upon her, she slipped her foot from the stirrup and slid down from her mount. Turning to Pride, she handed the mare's reins to him.

"Let me escort you to that small copse over there. Best we take advantage of the shade. Hopefully, we'll be out of earshot." He took her elbow and guided her across the field.

No further words passed between them as they walked towards the small group of pine trees. She opened her mouth to speak, but the words wouldn't come out. When they reached the trees, they stood and stared at each other for several long moments.

Bella broke eye contact first. She had come so far, there was no way back. She risked her future, but had to speak. "I've considered your offer—"

"My offer?" He folded his arms defensively across his chest. He looked bemused and leaned back against a tree.

Bella felt her colour rise. She took a few aimless paces, looking this way and that. Her heart beat quickened, her breathing became uneven, and she grasped her riding crop with both hands.

Acutely aware that her every move was being scrutinized, not only by Quentin but also by his men, who had stopped working, she looked up at him. He appeared calm. Being watched obviously caused him no apparent discomfort. She assumed he was accustomed to his crew following his every move while awaiting his decision. At sea, their lives depended upon their captain.

"Your marriage proposal," she said softly. She caught a flash of his blue eyes as she spoke.

"Ah," he raised an interested eyebrow but kept his arms folded. "If I recall, you said that you had long resolved not to marry."

"I believe I used those words."

"But you declined my offer. So, what offer have you come to discuss?"

"Perhaps if I hinted that I had changed my mind and would be prepared to consider offers of marriage in a more favourable light." There, she had said it. Anxiously she gazed up at him, expecting him to renew his proposal. He didn't reply. After a few painful moments, she tore her gaze away. How could this man, whom she had the deepest feelings for, be so exasperating? She turned again to face him and fixed her eyes on his. "You asked me to be your wife, and I said I wasn't planning to marry. Well, I have reconsidered and my answer would be the opposite." Believing she had given him sufficient grounds to renew his proposal, again she waited for his reply.

He remained silent.

They stood staring at each other for several long moments. On his every breath, she expected him to renew his offer. When he didn't, acute embarrassment welled up inside her like a huge wave. It washed through her and took away every scrap of confidence she had left. She turned away.

"Miss Richmond, could you explain why we should marry?"

His question surprised her, but as she had taken it upon herself to speak openly to him, she felt she owed him a truthful answer. "We're well-matched. Our family interests are similar. My father likes you."

"And you? What of your feelings on the matter?"

"Haven't I explained?"

"No."

"But I'd hardly be standing here, probably making a complete fool of myself, if I didn't want...if my feelings hadn't changed substantially."

"True," he nodded. He moved towards her and unfolded his arms.

She thought that he intended to wrap them around her and kiss her in full view of his crew. Readying herself, she dropped her riding crop.

He took a step towards her and put his hands behind his back, as if he was on the quarter-deck of his frigate. "Bella, as we are in private, may I call you so?"

"Please," she breathed, "if I may venture to call you Ross?"

"Agreed. Now that we have a more intimate understanding perhaps we can reach an agreement on a particular matter?"

Her heart pounded rapidly. Her madcap adventure to ride out to confront him ebbed towards success.

Excitement rose within her. He was about to renew his proposal. "Please continue."

"I have thought deeply and believe I understand your fear of loneliness when I return to my command."

His words were unexpected. She continued to gaze into his eyes hoping his next words would bring her ultimate joy.

"I spent the greater part of my early years in India, where my father had served with the army. He went to the Americas to fight for King George when the colonists declared independence. My mother, whom I can barely remember, insisted on following him. Her ship foundered. My father, bereft on hearing the news, blamed himself for allowing her to embark on a dangerous voyage solely for the purpose of joining him. He regarded his action as selfish. Now can you see why I have never allowed wives to accompany my officers? The service might deprive a child of one parent, but I'll not be responsible for the loss of both."

Conflicting emotions ebbed and flowed like the tide inside her. "I don't know what to say."

"I firmly believe that a wife's place is at home, especially when she has children. At home is where I expect my wife to remain. I understand that a marriage involving long periods of separation may not be to your satisfaction. So, despite the feelings we may have for each other, we face a situation which we cannot easily resolve to our mutual benefit." He glanced across at his men, then back to Bella. "And certainly not in the middle of a field while being scrutinized by twenty pairs of eyes."

As embarrassment engulfed her, she felt her mouth dry. She swallowed deeply and tried to salvage a small measure of dignity. Why had she acted so impetuously?

"I believe we should both reconsider, however difficult that may be. Bella, please understand that we must not allow emotion to triumph over prudent judgment."

He was sending her away! The thought cracked like a whip in her head. Her prime instinct was to run off and hide. How had she made such a terrible mistake? Did he believe a happy marriage between them would be impossible? It was not what she wanted to hear.

"Bella, forgive me for speaking bluntly, but it must be said. I have no doubt we could share a few happy months. However, once the peace is broken, I shall return to my command, and you will have to stay ashore. And that is my position."

From somewhere, she knew not where, she found the strength to hold her ground and look up at him. "Perhaps one day we might find a compromise. Until then, please accept my most sincere apologies for wasting your time. Goodbye, Captain Quentin."

She strode to where Pride held the horses. Without looking back at Ross she mounted and kicked Merriweather to a gallop. Once more, Pride was left to trail behind his mistress.

Bella didn't look back because she didn't want to give Quentin the satisfaction of seeing her tears. Perhaps he was right. Could she endure the months or even years of solitude? She didn't know, but her feelings for him were unchanged.

At that moment, she felt she couldn't possibly face him. Yet, the thought of never seeing Quentin again was abhorrent. And what would the neighbourhood think? She knew her behaviour would warrant comment. Well-brought up young ladies didn't go chasing men around the countryside in full view of estate workers.

What stories about her and the captain would be spread via the inn? More tears welled up inside her. She felt like a ship without a helmsman, being tossed on an open sea of broken dreams and regret. Why hadn't she had the patience to wait for him to come to her? He was a natural leader and strong enough to match her mercurial will. They were well-matched.

"Badly done, Bella, badly done." She cursed herself for her poor judgment as she let the mare have her head.

The tower of the parish church appeared from behind a swathe of trees. Not wanting to attract attention by arriving in the village at a full gallop, she slowed Merriweather to an easy trot. The wind had dried her tears. She drew a small lace handkerchief from her sleeve and blew her nose. Her eyes were sore and she knew her face was blotched. People would gossip if they saw how upset she was. She struggled for control of her feelings, but to no avail.

As she entered the village, she hoped no one would stop her to enquire after the admiral. She didn't want to speak to anyone. Fortunately, only a few heads turned as she trotted down the high street. A few estate workers tipped their hats as she passed by. She acknowledged them with a simple nod. At the church, she tethered Merriweather and strolled towards the gravestones. Sinking to her knees, a volcano of disappointed hopes and feelings, some instilled in her during childhood, erupted within her. Clasping her stomach, she bent double and wept bitterly.

* * * *

Ross watched Miss Richmond gallop away across the meadow until she was no more than a speck in the distance. His feelings churned inside him like a turbulent sea. He paced around the small copse, hands on his hips, trying to make sense of what had passed between them. He saw her discarded riding crop. He crouched to retrieve it and held it close to his chest, as if the contact meant he could hold her for a few more moments. He loved her. He didn't want to let her go. Somehow he had to find mutual ground upon which they could amicably settle. He decided to call upon her tomorrow.

Their encounter had left a bitter taste in his mouth. When he emerged from the copse twenty pairs of eyes stared back at him. "Back to work," he shouted, "and put your backs into it, lads!"

He toiled with his men for most of the afternoon until the work was finished. On his signal, the barrier holding the water back was knocked out. Water gushed along the channel. If the diversion prevented flooding in the lower meadow and increased the arable land, he would be satisfied with his day's work. The physical exertion should have kept his mind off Miss Richmond. It hadn't.

When his concentration had waned, or he had paused to rest, peace had eluded him. Her face was before him. Her disturbance of his domain had rattled him. He resented her invasion in the same way he disliked female interference on board his ship. And that was the irony. He wanted her more than any women he had ever known, but the sea was his mistress. He was not ready to settle permanently on land. He wanted to marry Miss Richmond provided she understood the lot of a sailor's wife.

The life he offered her was the life her mother had lived. The admiral never took his wife to sea. Ross shared Admiral Richmond's belief that a warship was no place for a wife. A sailor needed a home and the knowledge that his children had their mother to comfort them. He did not want his children abandoned to servants and tutors, as he had been.

He had confirmed his love for her. He wanted her then, physically and emotionally. And that troubled him. He could no longer trust himself alone with her. It kept him awake at night and tested his virtue, duty, and honour to the very limit. He loved her and, because he loved her, wanted to marry her. But could he knowingly subject her to the loneliness a marriage to him might entail?

He knew he had treated her badly, and he was ashamed of his behaviour. The only justification he could give for his action was it had been his last line of defence. He had to maintain self-discipline, but he was dangerously close to the breaking point. How easily he could have scooped her up in his arms and kissed her. And that would have given his crew even more to talk about.

* * * *

Bella entered Witton Abbey through the kitchen. She confirmed the dinner arrangements with the cook and took the back stairs to her bedchamber. She did not want to encounter Lady Mary because her friend would instantly know that something was wrong.

From her bedchamber, she glanced into the garden below. Lady Mary was walking alone. She stepped back from the window, still feeling very fragile from her encounter with Ross, and not wanting to be seen. Lady Mary and her father had become very close of late. They had been friends for several years since Captain Rufford had sailed with the admiral's flotilla in the West Indies. From the day the admiral had been incapacitated, and Lady Mary had come to stay at Witton, they had spent many hours in each other's company.

Often Bella had passed the sickroom and heard snippets of their lively conversation. Her father was always saying, "According to Lady Mary—" Sometimes he forgot himself and referred to her without her title. She wondered whether that was an indication of the extent of their friendship.

Had he thought of Lady Mary when he raised the idea of marrying again? Initially, the notion had surprised her, but as she mulled it over, she couldn't understand why she hadn't thought of it before. When her father was on his feet, Lady Mary would make an ideal new mistress of Witton Abbey. Bella's active mind raced ahead. Once her friend was installed at Witton, she would be free to marry.

"And what happens when he goes back to sea?" She asked the reflection glaring back at her from the cheval mirror. The question hung like a huge black cloud over her. "Well, are you strong enough to cope?"

Steadfastly she stood her ground and, staring back at herself, declared, "I love him, I always will, and I'm going to win him. Whatever it takes!"

* * * *

As Ross unsaddled Warrior, he heard the sound of another horse entering the yard. He gave the stallion over to one of his men and went outside to see who it was. He filled with elation when he saw Jeremy. They greeted each other with a hearty handshake. "I had no notion we would meet again so soon. You are a very welcome sight."

"You look as though you've been through a hedge backwards!" Jeremy pointed to the mud clinging to Ross's shirt, pantaloons, and boots.

Ross looked down at himself and laughed. "A drainage ditch needed re-enforcing. The land can be a hard mistress."

"I thought we claimed that for the sea!" Jeremy looked around him, softened his tone and said, "I need to speak with you privately. It's urgent. I've come direct from town."

Ross nodded and looked down at his clothes again. "I'm in need of a bath. But you, good friend, must have been in the saddle the best part of the day."

Jeremy nodded. "I left my manservant back on the road. I expect him with the spare horses, hopefully, before nightfall."

"Come to the house. You haven't ridden from town to pass the day in my stables." Upon entering the kitchen Ross called to Jackson, "Roll out two of the empty barrels and fill them with hot water. I'm aching from work on the land, and I'm sure my good friend is stiff from the saddle."

It wasn't long before both men had stripped off their clothes and slipped up to their armpits in the soothing water.

"Do you see, Jeremy, the advantage of an all male household? Bet you can't do this in your father's kitchen, eh?"

"Nor anywhere else in polite society, except on board ship." Jeremy rubbed the hard block of soap to get a lather.

"God Bless His Britannic Majesty's Navy, eh?"

"I'd prefer to toast the service with something stronger than a tub of suds." Jeremy dipped his head into the water to rinse his hair.

"Jackson," Ross shouted, "brandy!"

Swiftly the steward produced two glasses of the captain's best French.

"To your very good health, Jeremy."

"And yours."

* * * *

Later, when they were alone together in the library, Jeremy explained what had brought him into Hampshire so hastily. "Sir Humphrey Westwood is dead. The night before last, he was found shot in the street outside his club."

From the tone of Jeremy's words Ross knew something was amiss. He sat bolt upright sensing trouble. "Murdered?"

Jeremy clenched his teeth. "Before I explain the circumstances of Sir Humphrey's death, there's something more important you should know. He'd been playing cards, and witnesses at the club claim that he wagered Aston Grange and lost."

"Lost? To whom?"

"My question exactly. Can you imagine my disbelief when I learned it was Granville Richmond?"

Ross leaned forward in his armchair on the other side of the fireplace from Jeremy, his hands on his knees. "So doubtless I can expect a visit from the gentleman?"

"Gentleman? That scoundrel deserves no such designation. He was boasting of his conquest inside the club while the poor fellow met his end within yards of the entrance."

"How? Footpads?"

Jeremy paled. "No, it is said by his own hand. Put a pistol to his head."

"Because he's lost this place?"

"Possibly, but it wasn't his only estate. You know the man was a gamester. Hell, there's not a gaming club in London whose tables he hasn't graced at some time during his life. It doesn't make sense. He'd lost the Grange, but he was still solvent."

"So what's being done about it? What action is being taken by Sir Humphrey's supporters and his heir?"

"The whole affair is under investigation and the magistrates informed. Expect an inquiry in due course. As for the estate, there'll be a legal challenge. Richmond has witnesses in the club. His case looks watertight. That's why I came down here to warn you. Undoubtedly, you'll soon receive a call from your new landlord, if only to gloat."

"My lease is legal until Lady Day. If he crosses my threshold, he'll find little welcome here. We know he's been found cheating before when he tried to get Sir Humphrey to wager the estate."

"Yes, but it was never proven since the wager was declared null and void."

"And what about the incident at Lady Mary's ball?"

"Again, no proof," Jeremy replied. "Who wants to be known for harbouring card cheats under their roof?

The clubs cover it up and pass the fellow up by refusing him entry. But there's always someone who's gullible enough to fall for a shady deal."

"But wasn't Sir Humphrey a seasoned gambler?"

"Yes, but his wife and eldest son were killed in a coaching accident earlier this year. He'd been gambling heavily ever since. His state of mind could have made him an easy target for a scoundrel like Richmond."

"The blackguard! But tell me all you know."

"After Sir Humphrey had put up the Grange and lost it, Richmond offered him another wager, a chance to win his entire estate back. Sir Humphrey accepted, but a note came for him and he stepped outside to speak to his agent. Of course there was quite a crowd gathered around the table. You know how it is when the stakes are high. Sir Humphrey left, but said he would be back shortly. A shot was heard; people rushed outside and found the body in the street."

"And there were no other witnesses outside?"

Jeremy shook his head. "Apparently not. The note was undoubtedly a ruse."

Ross put his hand to his chin. He needed to think over the facts Jeremy had presented to him. He got up and paced around the room. "It appears highly suspicious. Did you get an agent to report on Richmond?"

"Aye, I did. He traced his movements for a few days. Then the intelligence is less clear. Indeed, Richmond appears to tell different stories to different people and uses aliases."

"Let's sketch his movements from the day of the ball, which was a Tuesday. Richmond was at Witton and had been there for a few days. The following day I called in the afternoon, but I didn't see him."

"And I left you on Thursday. When I reached London, I engaged the services of an agent to follow Richmond, as you instructed me."

"On Friday I spoke to the admiral again. He was out on his estate with his steward. I'm fairly certain Richmond had quit the place by then. Indeed, the admiral gave me the impression that there had been a family disagreement. And the attempt on the admiral's life was on Saturday. When did your agent first report Richmond in London?"

"Not until the following Monday evening, but it doesn't mean he wasn't there."

"True, it's too easy to jump to conclusions. However, Richmond certainly stood to gain if his uncle had been killed."

"How?" Jeremy asked. "He might be the admiral's nearest male relation but isn't Miss Richmond the heiress?"

"He could be a trustee?"

Jeremy looked doubtful. "The admiral's no fool! Would you appoint a wastrel to look after your daughter's inheritance?"

"Of course not! So let's go back to the attack on the admiral. How does Richmond gain from the death of his uncle?"

"He doesn't as long as his cousin's alive. And if she marries, he's lost the lot since it will go to her husband or her issue."

Ross put his hand to his chin. "Sir Humphrey's death, how does he gain there?"

"He increases his chance of holding onto Aston Grange. Foul play might be suspected, but with Sir Humphrey dead, who'll challenge him?"

"Sir Humphrey's heir, do you know who he is?"

Jeremy nodded. "The youngest son, Jonathan Westwood, is captain of the *Grafton*. But she's in the Caribbean, so I doubt if news will reach Westwood for a few weeks."

"Then it will be a sad day for him when it does."

"Indeed, loss of family is hard enough to bear, but more so when you are at sea and miles from home."

Ross nodded and took a few moments to gather his thoughts. 'Our case against Richmond is rather thin. Courts require witnesses and evidence. All we have is supposition. But it doesn't change the facts. Someone took a shot at Admiral Richmond, Sir Humphrey Westwood appears to have taken his own life for whatever reason, and doubtless my new landlord will make an appearance here sooner or later, whoever he may be." Ross picked up the decanter of brandy and poured himself another glass. He walked over to his friend and offered him another drink.

"We're sailors," moaned Jeremy, as the honey coloured liquid entered his glass, "not investigators. Now, what progress are you making with Miss Richmond?"

"Whenever did the course of true love run smoothly?" Ross hunched his broad shoulders. "In truth, I think life was simpler when we were at sea."

* * * *

Early the next morning Bella considered riding but swiftly dismissed the idea. She might meet Ross. With her matrimonial campaign underway, she preferred their first meeting to be in company. However, if she received some indication from him that he wished to speak to her, she would meet him alone.

As she descended the stairs she met Lady Mary. "I'm about to check on father's progress, would you care to join me?"

"Of course, my dear, but I think he is losing patience with his treatment of late."

As they entered, the admiral bellowed at his valet. "Get me out of this bed and into another room. Fetch Middleton and Taylor. Together you can shift me to the breakfast table." When he saw that Bella and Lady Mary were in the room, he looked at them appealingly, "I'm bored with eating bits off a tray."

Bella took up her usual place at his bedside. "But, Papa, your back."

"There's nothing the matter with my back that a stout meal off a proper table won't cure."

When Middleton arrived with the valet and two other manservants to shift the admiral, Bella and Lady Mary went to the breakfast room. The men carried the admiral on a chair and under his command positioned him at the table. Bella watched him closely and noted the painful grimace on his face as his valet lifted his splinted leg onto a stool.

"Enough, leave me be!"

Bella turned to Lady Mary. "Try to convince Papa that he mustn't do too much."

"I shall do nothing of the sort. The longer the admiral languishes in bed, the more difficult it will be for him to recover. Muscles get weak when they're not used, despite what any physician may say. My husband used to order malingerers to be prized from their hammocks when we were at sea. It only encourages more sickness, he used to say."

The admiral grinned from cheek to cheek. "Good man, Captain Rufford, an excellent commander. He was held in respect by all. Stay abed and you'll catch something else."

Feeling that she couldn't argue against both of them, Bella let out a long sigh and almost wished she'd gone riding. She stayed long enough to ensure that her father had eaten a hearty breakfast. "If you'll excuse me, I have correspondence to deal with. I'll be in the small parlour, if needed."

Settled at her escritoire, she had only replied to three letters when Middleton knocked and entered the parlour. "A note came five minutes ago, Miss Richmond. The messenger refused to wait for a reply."

"Thank you, Middleton." She took the sealed note from the salver. "I have several letters to send this morning, if this note requires a reply, I'll include it with the rest. That will be all." She heard him close the door, but her attention was on the letter. The direction read, "Miss A. Richmond." She broke the seal, and her heart leapt. It was from Ross.

Aston Grange,

Dear Miss Richmond,

Pardon the freedom with which I demand your attention, but I am desirous of seeing you again. Please meet me at the fork in the Turnpike Road, under the old chestnut tree at noon.

Your faithful and obedient servant,
Ross Quentin

The note was simple. The olive branch she craved; although he made no direct reference to their previous meeting, she hoped the outcome would be favourable to both parties. Ecstatic at the prospect of reaching an understanding between them, she rushed from the room. "Send word to the stables to saddle Merriweather and call my maid," she instructed Middleton as she hurried upstairs.

* * * *

"The mare's ready for you, Miss." Pride doffed his hat as she strode into the stable-yard. "Young Watson will accompany you, Miss. He's been chewing at the bit for a chance to give the new gelding his head."

Surprised Bella took a swift look at the new horse. "Did my father buy him?"

"No, Miss, but a horse dealer in the village two days ago heard we might need to replace the mare. We've got an option for a month. If he doesn't suit, he can go back."

"He's a fine animal, but I can't see the admiral riding a young gelding. Sadly it might be some time before he's back in the saddle."

"Yes, Miss, but you'll find young Watson will be able to keep up with you today. The cob's best kept for farm work."

Bella nodded her agreement and gently caressed the gelding's nose. She gave him a friendly pat on the neck. "I'll look forward to trying him, when he's ready to take a side-saddle."

Watson had a broad grin on his face as he led Merriweather out and helped his mistress up into the saddle. With the deft movement of youth, he mounted the gelding and followed his mistress. Bella galloped towards the turnpike road which ran north to south and separated the two estates. At the edge of Chestnut Wood, a fork in the road led to the village. Filled with anticipation, she could barely contain her excitement as she neared their rendezvous.

Quentin had asked her to come to him. Could he see a future for them together? She secretly hoped that today she would hear the renewal of his proposal. That somehow he had found mutual ground upon which they could build their future life together. She had no idea of where they would call home, but it didn't seem to matter to her anymore. She was on her way to the man she loved. She urged Merriweather to go faster.

At the fork in the road, she reined in and waited beneath the branches of the chestnut tree. She glanced about her, but there was no sign of Ross or his stallion. Perhaps she was early?

She smiled and chided herself for being too eager. She let the mare walk on, to cool her down from her gallop. Clear of the woods, she looked up and from the position of the sun decided it was nearly noon. Turning to the young groom, she asked, "How goes the gelding?"

He doffed his hat. "Very fair, Miss Richmond."

"Suitable for the admiral?"

"That I dunno. This gelding's a lively beast and needs a firm hand."

"Do you think he'd take a side-saddle?"

"We could try him in the paddock, Miss. If Mr. Pride agrees, I'd be willing to school him for you."

"Have you ever ridden a lady's saddle?"

"No, Miss, but I'd be happy to try with the gelding if that's what's wanted."

"You're—"

A shot rang out. Merriweather reared. Expertly, Bella battled to control her. Out of the corner of her eye, she saw Watson slumped forwards as the gelding bolted into the woods.

Instinct drove her. Kicking her mare to a gallop, she pursued the runaway horse and rider. Twisting and turning, dodging branches, she fought to keep sight of them. With a heavy thud, the gelding deposited his rider in the undergrowth. She reined in, slid from her saddle, and secured Merriweather's straps to a nearby tree.

Crouched at Watson's side, she saw blood oozing from his shoulder. His face had turned white, his were blue, and he made no sound. Was he dead or alive?

"Watson!" She searched for any sign that the boy still lived. Holding her fingers to his neck, she fumbled for his pulse. At the sound of a branch snapping behind her, she whipped her head around. Dark shadows blocked out the noonday sun. Hands grabbed her and wrenched her away from the wounded youth.

Her hat and veil were torn from her and replaced by a foul-smelling bag pulled over her head. She struggled to breathe in the darkness. Powerful arms swept around her torso and restrained her in an iron-like grip.

Terrified, she screamed loudly. Kidnapped! It was happening again. She kicked against her oppressors with every ounce of resistance that she had in her body. But they were too strong for her. Her arms were pulled behind her back, her wrists bound, and her ankles and knees restrained with rope. More canvas was wrapped around her body until she must have resembled a body ready for sea burial. Swept off her feet, she was thrown over a man's shoulder and carried a short distance. Flung onto a hard surface, she winced from the impact and blacked out.

Chapter Thirteen

Ross worried about Granville Richmond's acquisition of Aston Grange. The affair seemed tainted with skulduggery and, possibly, murder. As he rode to Witton, another important matter played on his mind. He felt ashamed of his behaviour to Bella the previous day. He had been very crass. She had surprised him by seeking him out while he laboured at the drainage ditch with his men.

It had taken a great deal of courage on her part, and her feelings for him must be very strong. Yet, he wasn't convinced she was ready to be a sailor's wife. As he neared Witton, he decided to pay his respects to the admiral before speaking to Bella. When he had her alone, he would apologize and ask for her forgiveness. If her feelings towards marriage had changed, as she had implied, and she understood he would return to his command when war broke out, he would renew his proposal.

It was a simple plan, but he doubted it would be plain sailing.

"Have you seen Miss Richmond, Captain?" Pride asked as he grasped Warrior's bridle.

"No, is she out riding?"

"Yes, Captain. She went out with young Watson over two hours ago. Thought you might have seen them on your way here. The lad's trying out a new gelding we've been offered."

For a brief moment, Ross considered riding to meet her. However, as he had business with the admiral, he dismounted and went to find him. Middleton greeted him at the main entrance. "Admiral Richmond has removed to the library."

The news that the admiral had left the sickroom pleased Ross. As he entered the library to be announced, he found the admiral sitting in a large armchair, his injured limb propped up on a long stool. Lady Mary was keeping him company while applying her needle to a small piece of embroidery. Having greeted them with the usual formalities, Ross related the incident concerning Sir Humphrey Westwood and revealed the identity of his new landlord.

The admiral's face dropped. "He'll not take possession. The man's got too many creditors. They'll want their cut before Granville can get his feet under the table. He'll have to sell."

As the admiral spoke, Middleton re-entered the room and positioned himself close to his master. When the admiral had finished, he spoke in a low voice to him.

"What? Speak out man," the admiral cried. "This is for all our ears."

"Pride is in the hall. Miss Richmond's mare has returned to the stables without her."

Ross jumped to his feet. "With your permission, sir, I'll organize a search party. Did she say where she was riding to?"

The admiral shook his head. "I've no idea! I didn't know she had gone riding. No one tells me anything!"

Lady Mary stood up. "When did she leave and where has she gone?"

"Excuse me, sir," Middleton coughed. "Miss Richmond left about two hours ago. There was a note for her earlier. The messenger was a rough looking fellow. He said he'd come from the Grange. I thought the note was from you, Captain."

"Note? I sent no message to Miss Richmond this morning. Middleton, where was Miss Richmond when you delivered this note?"

"Miss Richmond was in the small parlour at her writing desk. She seemed very pleased to receive it, sir."

Without saying a word, Lady Mary dashed out of the library.

"I don't like this," the admiral said. "There have been too many incidents in the neighbourhood for this to be another accident."

"We need her destination or some clue to her direction." Ross turned to Middleton, "Who rode with her?"

"I don't know, sir."

"Get Pride in here, at once!" the admiral said.

Lady Mary rushed back through the open door, clutching a piece of paper. "Bella has gone to the turnpike road to meet you, Captain Quentin. Is this your hand?"

Ross glanced quickly at the sheet of paper and shook his head. "There's more to Bella's disappearance than being unseated from her mare." He turned to Pride. "What's happened to her groom?"

"We don't know, sir. He went out with Miss Richmond, and he wouldn't have left her. It's more than his life's worth!"

"And I'll have his life if he's let any harm come to my daughter! Quentin, take every available man and all the horses. Start searching the turnpike road. Turn out the dogs. Blast this damned leg!" the admiral bellowed.

"Aye aye, sir. I'll go straight to Chestnut Wood and begin the search at the fork," Ross said. "Middleton, send word to the Grange. Mr. Thwaite came last night; he will lead my crew. Sir, if you could coordinate the search and relay messages to the various parties, we'll ensure our efforts aren't duplicated."

"Yes, of course. Keep me informed. Middleton, supply the captain with flags and put a signaller on the roof."

Ross addressed the admiral. "I fear someone lured Miss Richmond into a trap. Perhaps the same villains who held up her coach and tried to shoot you, sir."

The admiral shook his head. "God forbid. Go to it, lad. I know you'll not leave a stone unturned until she's found."

"What can I do?" Lady Mary asked.

Both men glanced anxiously at each other.

"Question all the servants," Ross replied, "especially the maids. Find out if anyone saw anything or if anybody in the neighbourhood has been acting suspiciously. Prepare a sickroom with fresh linen and bandages. Ensure that the cook has food ready for the returning search parties. We'll all need feeding."

He turned to the admiral. "Where are the estate plans?"

* * * *

Bella woke with a start. She blinked several times; there was no light, just darkness. She moved her head and wished she hadn't. It hurt. The canvas bag covering her face reeked of mould. She thought she was being conveyed in a vehicle. The cart, or wagon, jostled her body and the wheels rattled as if going over stony cobbles. She struggled to remember what had happened, but her head throbbed.

She remembered hitting something hard after they had trussed her up in the canvas. Her shoulder and left knee ached, her elbows were sore, and her head pounded. Had she collided with an object, or had one of her captors hit her? Desperately, she tried to remember what had happened. *Think quickly*, she told herself. This time her abduction was planned. Someone had lured her to Chestnut Woods. Ross? No, that was impossible.

Where was she? Where were they taking her? And who were they? Too many questions.

Calm down!

She listened intently to the sounds around her. The rattling of the vehicle's wheels over cobbled ground suggested a village, or from the muddle of sound, a town.

Her hands and ankles were bound fast, but she was alive. If someone wanted to take her life, they would have already done the deed. But what had happened to Watson? His pale face flashed before her. He'd been wounded, she was certain of that. She prayed he was still alive. And Ross? Where was he? She had dismissed the notion that he was responsible for luring her to the meeting place. He couldn't have written the note, but who had?

The vehicle stopped. Memory of her previous abduction flooded back. Were these captors the same men? Whoever they were, they had rendered her unconscious. She decided to appear as if she was still unconscious, hoping they would not hurt her again. Escape was not feasible at present. She needed time to think, to calculate risk, and to discover who wanted to do her harm.

The nagging image of Watson splayed on the ground persisted, accompanied by a flash of her father similarly brought down. Had the sharpshooter found his target this time? Had he immobilized Watson to abduct her?

Close by, she heard men begin to speak rapidly. The language sounded French, but she only understood a few words. Was it some sort of dialect? That would explain why it sounded so familiar without being at all comprehensible. Hands grabbed her ankles and began dragging her across the bed of the vehicle. She couldn't see through the canvas hood and had no idea who was taking her.

Hands grabbed her body and handled her roughly, like a plague victim for whom they had little respect. She wanted to cry out but bit down on her lip. The solidity of a male shoulder creased her stomach and she knew she was being carried aloft. Fear consumed her, fear of the unknown. Her hands began to shake, her throat dried, and every breath she took smelled foul.

She craned her ears for any sound that would give a clue to her location. They must have taken her into a building, she reasoned, since the sounds of the streets, horses, carriage wheels, and cries of sellers had dulled. Silently, she prayed they wouldn't throw her into water or some evil pit from which escape would be impossible. Her fears did not abate, but she forced her body to stay limp.

The man carrying her put her down, and she heard footsteps retreating. She waited, sweating profusely in the humid atmosphere. Her hearing became sensitized to every sound and movement around her. When she heard the scratching of rats, she knew she was alone. The sound, which she normally would have shied away from, brought her welcome relief. Knowing her captors had left, she let out a deep sigh.

Slowly she brought her knees up to her chest. With great effort, she squeezed her pelvis and legs through her tied arms. With her hands in front of her, she managed to make a hole in the bag covering her head and brought her wrists to her mouth. Ignoring thirst and hunger, she began gnawing through the ropes which bound her.

* * * *

"Over here!"

Ross heard the call and rushed to where the men stood gathered around the injured youth, concern etched on their faces. "Miss Richmond?" He dropped on one knee beside the lad. "What happened to her?"

Watson's pale face creased. "I dunno, sir." His voice was but a whisper. "My shoulder. Horse bolted. Guess I fell off."

"That you did, lad. Let Mr. Pride examine your wound."

Pride knelt down and supported Watson's arm as he turned the boy over to inspect his back. "You're lucky, boy. The ball's gone straight through."

Watson grimaced, his face pale, his lips blue. "What? I don't understand, sir."

"You've been shot, Watson." Ross looked quizzically at Pride. The head groom's expression did not bode well for the boy. "Can you remember anything?"

The lad screwed up his face. "She was screaming...calling out my name. I was face down. Then darkness. Two men in long dark coats. They turned me over, but the pain was agony. They said something. I couldn't understand. They weren't English. I'm sorry, sir, I don't remember."

Pride looked anxiously at the captain. "He's very weak. I'll do my best to staunch the bleeding."

"Do what you can for him, but don't move him. I'll send to Portsmouth for Dr. Grey." Satisfied that Watson had no further information, Ross ordered men to return to Witton with the news. He gave instructions concerning medical supplies and where to contact the surgeon in Portsmouth. Although there was no sign of Bella, he organized men into search teams to cover the area. Increasingly he feared that Bella had been abducted, or worse.

Thought of her demise triggered a wave of nausea to well up from his stomach and leave a bitter taste in his mouth. So much so that he refused to think the worst again. There would be time for grieving and remorse when he had the evidence before him. He needed no further confirmation of his feelings for her. He loved her.

Meanwhile, one of the search parties found disturbed ground with downtrodden bracken and threads of dark navy velvet caught on brambles. Finally, the matching riding hat and veil were also recovered.

"What do you make of it?" Ross asked Walters, the admiral's steward who had found the spot.

"Foul play, Captain," he answered. "Miss Richmond was unhorsed, or she got down to help Watson. There's been a struggle, all right, and I think they left that way." He pointed towards the likely route.

"They?"

"Yes, Captain, *they*," Walters replied. "Two men, maybe three, and they had a cart or a carriage with thick wheels. They'd pulled off the turnpike road and had been waiting awhile. They left with Watson's horse tied to the back. The tracks are quite clear and they went south."

"South?" Ross asked, glancing along the road. "There's only one reason to go south from here."

"Portsmouth," the men added in unison.

* * * *

Ross rode Warrior at a full gallop back to Witton, where he found Jeremy with the admiral and Lady Mary in the library. He'd left the rest of the men, mostly estate workers, behind to follow on foot. Pride had been tasked with Watson's care until the surgeon arrived.

Having explained his findings, Ross added: "I believe she's been kidnapped."

"Kidnapped!" the admiral said. "By those damned Frenchies again?"

"We don't know, sir," Ross said. "If someone had wanted her life, then they would have taken it when they had the opportunity. Instead, they took her with them."

The admiral breathed in sharply. "Do they intend to ransom her?"

"Possibly, that's why it's vital for you to remain here, sir, where any potential demand is likely to be made."

"I see, Quentin," he nodded. "Damn this injured leg and damn their eyes if they harm my daughter."

Ross turned to Lady Mary and Jeremy. "Any news from your enquiries?"

Lady Mary nodded. "One of the kitchen maids said her sister had heard stories of an engagement between Miss Richmond and yourself, Captain. She said two strangers at the inn last night had remarked that their master wouldn't be pleased to hear the news, as he planned to marry the lady."

"Mary, did these strangers say who they were working for?" the admiral asked.

"No, Henry, but the maid's sister described them as strangers because of their odd accents. They spoke poor English. She thought they might be French. Many foreigners have been through these parts of late, so she didn't think anymore of it until this afternoon."

"Are these men still at the inn?" Jeremy asked. "Only they sound very similar to ones I had described to me by some farm labourers."

"I've been told they left early this morning," Lady Mary replied.

"I have a description of two men wearing boat cloaks," Jeremy added. "Rather hot for this time of the year, but stout protection against the elements. They have been in the neighbourhood for about ten days. One of them carries a long French musket."

"That description might fit dozens of men." Ross paced the room and dragged his hand through his hair. "Finding those two men in Portsmouth will be worse than looking for a needle in a haystack. We must begin the search immediately, but we've so little intelligence."

The admiral sat quietly, deep in thought. He looked directly up at Ross. "The only proposal I am aware of my daughter receiving was from her cousin, and she sent him packing!"

Ross looked knowingly at Jeremy, who nodded slightly, but neither said anything.

"Damn Granville," the admiral grumbled. "Whenever there is something amiss, he's somewhere about."

"Precious time is being lost," Ross said. "We have gathered as many men as we can muster. Thwaite and I will search Portsmouth. As soon as we find her, we'll send word."

"Quentin," the admiral beckoned him over to his chair. "If they've taken her south, it's to board ship. If you have to give chase, take my sloop, the *Vesta*. She's decommissioned but still sea-worthy." He looked at Lady Mary and said, "Give me pen and paper to write my authority. Quentin needs written orders."

* * * *

A stiff easterly breeze turned the crowded anchorage of Portsmouth harbour into a haphazard pattern of whitecaps. Anchored ships, mostly laid up for the peace, bobbed up and down, unmanned and uncared for. Through the eyes of an experienced captain, the fleet looked in a sorry state.

"Have you found the *Diana*?"

"Yes." Ross collapsed his glass and offered it to Jeremy. "The sight of her does not gladden my heart."

Jeremy extended the instrument and ran it over the frigate from bow to stern. "I've seen the old girl looking better."

"Let's hope this isn't a bad omen."

"Since when has bad luck bothered you, Ross?"

"Since I met the *Diana's* rival. Do you remember I asked you where I could find a woman to match my frigate for dash, style, and courage?"

"You've found her, haven't you, Ross?"

"Yes, and every waking minute I pray I've not lost her."

Diligently they scoured every inn, tavern, and boarding house in the seaport. At sunset Ross and his search parties met up at the Blue Post Inn at Portsmouth Point. The landlord recognized the captain instantly, wiped a table, and offered his best victuals.

"Can you feed and board my men?" Ross asked, knowing it was usually young gentlemen who lodged there, not ordinary seamen.

"Yes, Captain, that'd be no trouble. I'm right glad of the trade. Most of the middies have gone back to their homes, those that have got them. Of course, the others, they've all got light pockets, ain't they? I curse the day the peace broke out, sir, if you don't mind me saying. Why, I'd almost be grateful if Boney did invade. At least the Admiralty would have to wake up and man the ships. They are a sorry sight for any sailor's eyes. It's enough to make you weep. The pride of His Britannic Majesty's Royal Navy is at anchor and not one of them ready to put to sea."

A serving girl placed two pots of steaming food on the table.

"Two glasses of brandy," Jeremy ordered.

The landlord nodded. "Stew for the men, sir? The Missus ain't making the rabbit pie, unless it's ordered special."

Ross nodded and began tucking into the thick stew. He had no idea what sort of meat he was eating and thought it best not to ask.

His meal was interrupted by a commotion at the door. Jackson pushed his way into the inn dragging another man by his collar. "Excuse me, Captain."

Jackson stood over the man who looked as if he'd recently taken a beating.

"What's the meaning of this?" Ross asked, looking at the man, who fell on his knees.

"Captain," Jackson said, "this piece of scum has been working for the Frenchies. Oh, he's been turned on shore by the service, like the rest of us, and says he needed the money for his family, but that ain't no excuse for what he's been doing!"

Ross stood up and hauled the man to his feet. "What your name?"

"Turner, sir."

"Jackson, what does he stand accused of?"

"He's been piloting a French vessel, smuggling brandy, but even worse they've been taking young girls and selling them to the pirates off the North African coast. Hanging from the yard-arm's too good for the likes of him!"

"Piloting a French vessel is no crime, now we are at peace with the French. As for smuggling brandy, you'll answer to the customs men for that, but kidnapping! That's a hanging offence."

"Not guilty, sir," Turner blurted out. "As soon as I knew what those Frenchies were really up to, I didn't go anywhere with them except the French coast a few times. And when I heard what they'd been doing with the young women, I quit. You've got to believe me, Captain. They wanted me to go to some village inland with them. Said they'd got a special job for some English merchant to take a young woman to France, and it had to be done today. We only heard about it last night."

Ross grabbed the man by his coat. "Who is she? What was the name of the village?"

"I don't know her name, but we had to take her at noon today, somewhere north of here on the turnpike road. But I didn't go with them, honest. Captain, I've been at home all day with my family."

"My God, Ross, it could be Miss Richmond!" Jeremy said.

Turner shook his head. "I didn't know her name, and I didn't go with them, I jumped ship yesterday. I swear it."

"And the vessel? What's her name? Where is she now?"

"She's the *Marie Claire* and her captain's name is Artois. She sailed on the evening tide for Brest."

* * * *

Through the hole she had made in the sail bag, Bella saw an enclosed room with heavily timbered walls. It was probably a store or warehouse of some kind since the objects around her included ropes, bundles of canvas, barrels, and pulleys. She guessed it was a chandlery.

Although she had tried to chew her way through the rope which bound her wrists, she had failed. The hemp had left a bitter taste in her mouth. Her feet also remained tied. As the light faded, she thought of Watson and wondered whether his young life had been taken. And what were her captors planning to do with her?

Heavy footsteps approached, accompanied by gruff voices. She feigned unconsciousness and listened intently. The men were still speaking in a French dialect which she had difficulty understanding. They laughed, and she felt herself lifted and carried over a man's shoulder.

Where were they taking her now? Inside the bag she tried to breathe slowly, afraid that even the slightest sound from her would trigger violence from them. The man who carried her spoke to his companion. She listened to their voices, convinced there were no more than two of them.

The men stopped talking, but the thud of their boots on wood persisted. The thug carrying her tightened his grip as he jolted her, as if transporting her over a challenging pathway or down steps. Another voice called out, and the man closest to her shouted back. He put her down, but she didn't know where.

The air smelled different. A mixture of pungent aromas invaded her nose; salt beef, tar, bilge, and brandy. She peered through her peep hole—blackness. Either the light had faded, or she was inside a windowless room. She shivered, not from the cold, but with fear of the unknown. Everything seemed unreal in the darkness, until she heard the groaning of timber. Instantly she recognized the sound, and with it came an almost homely feeling. She was on board a vessel and the ship was underway.

* * * *

As dawn broke, the *Vesta* made sail with Ross in command and Jeremy as first lieutenant. Although Ross added his men to the skeleton crew kept by Admiral Richmond, the sloop was undermanned. The crew would have to work double shifts if he was to get maximum speed out of her. He prayed for a fair wind.

During the night, he learned from those who regularly kept watch and were prepared to sell information, that the *Marie Claire* was a French square rigged merchantman, but she looked more like a brig. He confirmed she had sailed on the evening tide and her lack of a cargo had drawn some notice. However, one piece of intelligence convinced Ross to give chase. The revenue men reported that a woman dressed in dark blue had been carried aboard the *Marie Clare*. When he asked why it hadn't been reported earlier, the officer replied, "If we chased every doxy who plies her trade on board ships, we'd have no time left to collect the King's Revenue."

To think that anyone could refer to Bella in those terms sickened Ross to his very core. He sent a message back to Witton reporting that she had possibly been sighted and they were setting sail for Normandy.

"It'll be good to be at sea again," Jeremy said when he joined his captain on deck.

"Yes," Ross replied. "I pray she is alive. If she is on board the *Marie Claire*, it's against her will." Silently he prayed they hadn't hurt her, but he feared that her strong character would not suffer captivity easily. He knew her well enough—she would resist. "Who's behind this?"

Jeremy shrugged. "I'd like to catch up with this English merchant who profits from selling young women into a lifetime of slavery. Is that why he wants Miss Richmond?"

"Perhaps, but I believe there is more behind her capture. She was deliberately lured away. The motive could be ransom or even revenge."

Jeremy shrugged his shoulders again. "Why take her on board if ransom is the motive? Why take her to

France? And revenge? That's an entirely different kettle of fish. Kidnap needs planning, a hideout, a method to collect the ransom, and an escape route. Somebody is behind this. They need contacts, intelligence, and opportunity to guarantee success. It appears highly improbable, but Granville Richmond springs to mind."

"Jeremy, in that we're of one mind. But why propose to her?" Ross paced the quarter deck. "Men like Richmond do not marry without attention to monetary advantage. He regards himself as the admiral's heir and expects to inherit his fortune. On discovering there is a trust for his cousin, he offers for her, gets rejected, and seeks revenge."

"Did *he* try to kill his uncle?"

Ross stood square with his hands on his hips. "I don't know. There is no proof. When Bella refused him, he might have wanted revenge. But killing the admiral would place Bella's fortune into the hands of her trustees. I doubt if Richmond is one of them. It would be too risky for him to let her inherit. But if he heard a rumour that she was engaged, he could not delay his plan. Once married, her husband would inherit the estate, and Witton would be lost to him for good."

"So what is Richmond's plan?"

"He might have the Grange, but men like him are greedy. He wants more. He wants Witton Abbey as well. How can he get it? Murder both his uncle and his cousin?"

"He'd pay lackeys to do his dirty work," Jeremy scoffed.

"I believe you're right. Richmond won't risk a noose. He thinks too much about his own welfare for that. But we must not underestimate him. Like the fox, he's cunning."

"If he has kidnapped Bella, what are his intentions?"

Ross thought awhile. "I believe he plans to marry her. She would never agree, so the ceremony would be under duress and therefore, invalid. Thus, he takes her abroad. On the Continent, he can bribe a town official and have the documentation in place without Bella knowing about it. He could imprison her and declare her insane. He might also arrange for an accident to befall her. The possibilities are numerous. When the time suits him, he returns to England with the sad news for his uncle. Who, grief-stricken, might be found like Sir Humphrey."

"By all the saints! The very notion makes my blood chill."

"The man may act the fop, but we know he's corrupt. Never underestimate your enemy, Jeremy, on land or at sea. It's the first lesson of warfare."

They weighed anchor, made sail, and slipped into the Channel.

"The bridge is yours, Jeremy," Ross said, making his way to the captain's cabin.

With the charts spread across the table, he plotted a course for Brest, his quarry's reported destination. As he worked, he realized what an enormous gamble he was taking. He had to catch the *Marie Claire*, board her in peace time and, if she was aboard, rescue Bella. If she wasn't—he daren't think about the consequences.

Bella heard the men approaching and tried to prepare herself for the worst. When they wrenched the canvas hood from her head, she gasped, afraid they had come to do her harm. By the dim candlelight of a single lantern, she came face to face with her abductors for the first time.

One man wielded a knife and freed her ankles. She hoped he'd also free her wrists, but he backed away and concealed his weapon about his person.

"Come," the other man snarled. "Come!" He grabbed her arm and hauled her to her feet.

"Water," she pleaded. "I need to drink." Her mouth felt so parched that she could hardly moisten her lips to swallow. Indifferent to her cries, the men forced her out of the empty hold and onto the open deck.

The ship tossed at the mercy of the rough sea and the wind howled. Bella shivered in the cold air. The biggest waves broke over the ship's prow, and smaller ones crashed against the hull. Realizing that the vessel was making little headway, Bella glanced up and saw how poorly rigged the ship was for the prevailing sea conditions. She blamed the captain and his sail master.

Looking up, she searched for some hint of how high the sun had risen. A dense patchwork of grey, rain-threatening clouds blanketed the sky. Convinced that the weather conditions would worsen before they improved, she began to fear for the ship's seaworthiness.

A speck on the horizon caught her eye. The slovenly sailors about her were either unaware of it or too lazy to do anything about it. They would soon need to trim their vessel, she decided, since the heavy clouds could easily bring a squall.

The two guards grabbed her arms and frog-marched her towards the stern. They pushed her into the quarters below the small orlop deck. A man sat behind a table. If he was the captain, he was a poor excuse for one. A round fellow, clad in seaman's garb, bald-headed and unshaven, he picked his grubby fingernails with a small knife. Despite the huge stern windows behind him, the cabin was dark. The panes of glass should have let plenty of light through, but they were filthy with grime and sea salt.

"Why have I been brought aboard this vessel against my will?"

"Ah, so proud. We had many like you during the Terror. So full of their own importance, until they tasted the prison cells and caught a whiff of Madame Guillotine."

"What do you want with me?" She asked, ignoring his comment about revolutionary France and softening her tone.

"I believe you're valuable to your father." He ran his eyes over her as if she were for sale.

"So you've kidnapped me for ransom?"

"I am Captain Artois," he declared proudly, "a merchantman. I have no desire to kidnap you."

"Why have I been brought here under duress?"

"Let us say I have a client. A gentleman who wants you transported to France and is prepared to pay a tidy sum to have you delivered there. Fortunately for you, he wants you alive!" He grinned, exposing blackened teeth.

"Indeed." Bella sniffed, determined not to let him intimidate her. Inwardly she breathed a sigh of relief. "I assume your role in this affair is purely mercenary?"

"But of course," he drawled. "Would I have anything to do with abduction? I merely provide passage for you to France for my client, and you will do well to remember that."

"So, I am here as your guest taking passage to France, am I?" She gave him a false smile. "How pleasant, Captain. I suggested a trip to the Continent to my father quite recently, but he didn't favour it. Now, untie my wrists and give me something to eat and drink."

Captain Artois chuckled. "You have spirit, my lady. I did not think you English women were so amusing." He stood up, sauntered around his table and stood in of front her. He drew a knife from the side of his boot.

Bella stepped back, afraid he was going to attack her. "Who are you working for?"

"You do not need to know, but he will not be a happy man if you come to harm." He grabbed her wrists and cut the bond between them. "Do not try to escape; my door is always guarded and you are at sea, so you have nowhere to go."

There was a sharp knock on the door. One of the henchmen stuck his head into the cabin. He spoke to his captain, informing him that a ship had been sighted. She tried to look pan-faced. The less they thought she understood the better.

"We have company." He flashed his black teeth at her, grabbed her upper arm, and dragged her around the table. "Sit down!"

Bella held onto the arms of the chair, grateful to have her hands freed. He tucked his knife back into the top of his boot, seized a length of rope, looped it around her waist, and tied her to the chair. "That'll keep you put."

He was so close she smelled garlic on his breath. "Food and drink?"

Artois picked up a glass from the mahogany cabinet at the side of the cabin. He poured wine from a decanter and offered it to her. Afraid that wine on an empty stomach would go straight to her head, she hesitated, but her throat felt as dry as dust. Reluctantly, she took the drink from him and bending, sipped it slowly, relieved to moisten her lips and tongue with the red liquid.

As she drank, Artois began fingering her blonde curls. "You're to be married, mam'selle. What a pity! My men and I mustn't touch!" He coughed, backed away from her, and spat phlegm onto the floor.

"Am I? This is news indeed. And who's the fortunate man?"

"Ah, that would be telling, wouldn't it?"

"My father will never give his permission. Besides, I thought Scotland was where irregular marriages took place, not France."

He shrugged. "I am only the deliverer of the bride. I think my client can manage without your father's say so."

Bella took a deep breath. She was determined not to show her fear, but she couldn't stop her heart racing. Hopefully, Captain Artois wouldn't notice how frightened she really was. There was a loud knock on the door and a seaman entered the cabin. He was wet through and dripped water on the floor. In French he asked the captain to come on deck. Artois grunted his annoyance and followed him.

The ship shifted violently to larboard, and loose items were flung across the cabin. Bella managed to anchor her feet under the captain's table, which was fixed to the deck. Tied to the chair, she hung on.

The roar of the wind grew louder, and waves continued to pound the ship's hull. The harsh weather was testing the sails and rudder, but especially the crew. Already pitching and with her timbers groaning, the *Marie Claire* began to roll.

Bella seized her chance. Poking her fingers through the back of the chair, she struggled to free herself. Digging her finger nails into the knot, she jiggled it, loosened the tension, and then pulled one end free. She tore the rope from around her waist, and leapt to her feet. The ship listed to starboard and the door swung open. She expected someone to enter the cabin, but there was no one there. Tentatively she made for the open doorway and peered out. The guard had gone. Her way was clear, so she slipped out of the cabin.

The strong winds had turned into a storm. The ship rolled and pitched. Driving rain drenched her decks. Bella found a boat cloak hanging on a peg. Hurriedly, she put it around her shoulders and hooked the chain across the front to secure it.

Out on the open deck, the situation was far worse than she had imagined. The fore, top, and mizzen mainsails flapped uncontrollably in the wind. She saw three men, including the captain, clinging to the wheel, fighting to get the ship to answer her rudder. She glanced over her shoulder to larboard, where she had sighted the other vessel earlier. Her heart gladdened. The ship running in their wake was her father's sloop, the *Vesta*.

Chapter Fourteen

"It's the *Marie Claire* all right," Jeremy shouted from the small quarterdeck, "and we're gaining on her."

"Is she flying any colours?" Ross asked, aware of the regulations under the Peace Treaty regarding firing on French vessels.

"None, Captain."

"Prepare the cannon. Gun crews to fire only on my signal. Take care, Mr. Thwaite. Today, we're privateers." Ross knew the coordination of cannon fire in rough seas was near impossible. But he had confidence in his men. He knew their calibre. They would fire at will if ordered to do so. "The sea's running fast, Mr. Thwaite. Secure the gun ports until the last minute."

"Aye aye, Captain."

"Glad for the taste of a skirmish?" Ross called after him.

"Yes, Captain." he saluted.

"Look, sir," one of the helmsmen cried. "She's raising the tri-colour."

Ross put his glass to his eye. "Damn!" he seethed. "Mr. Sanders, get me within firing range."

The sail master acknowledged the order, but cautiously eyed the French flag. "I'll do my best, but in this high sea?" He shook his head. "By the look of the Frenchie, she's got a load of land lubbers at her helm."

"My thoughts precisely, Mr. Sanders."

"Any rocks or shoals about, sir?"

"None to worry us at present, but you know these waters as well as most."

"I can't see Admiral Richmond being too pleased if his vessel comes to grief, sir."

"I've not lost a ship yet, Mr. Sanders," said Ross, "and I've no intention of losing this one."

"Yes, Captain."

* * * *

Half-hidden in the shadow of the *Marie Claire's* poop deck, Bella watched Captain Artois and the two men struggle with the wheel. The mainsail flapped wildly. Nearly torn from its yard, it was dragging them to larboard. The topsails were reefed, but the torn sail was pulling them over, no matter how much rudder was applied.

Artois bellowed orders in French, but no one answered him. The *Marie Claire* had all but run away from her crew. Undermanned, she was her own mistress and at the mercy of the sea.

Bella realized they had to strike the mainsail, or they would capsize. Under the cover of her borrowed cloak, she dashed to the tool box where the axes were stored. She held fast to a rope with one hand and wrenched open the lid with her other. Wedging the box open with her foot, she grabbed a hand axe.

As the sea crashed over the *Marie Claire's* deck, she waited to count the seconds between the waves. Taking her chance between the surges, she ran to the main mast. With all the strength she could muster, she began hacking through the main sheet in the driving rain. Two men, armed with axes, joined her. Fired by urgency to free the sail, together they severed the ropes.

The ship listed badly, her decks awash. Desperately, Bella clung on as she struggled to free yet another rope. The dreadful groan of timber splitting ground the length of the vessel. The yard gave way, broke from its lashing with the main mast, and crashed to the deck. The *Marie Claire* listed further. The wreckage acted as a sea anchor and the task to release the broken yard and mainsail became vital. A few more minutes and the ship would likely capsize.

Artois and his two helmsmen tied the wheel, raced to the deck, and began to clear wreckage. In the mayhem and drenched by the rain, Bella must have looked like another hand. No one stopped or questioned her, not even the captain.

Through the squall, she saw the *Vesta* had closed the distance between them. But Captain Artois flew the French Tri-colour. Bella tightened her grip on her axe and edged her way to the stern. With several adept blows, she cut through the rope and watched the panels of blue, white, and red fly off on the wind.

＊＊＊＊

"She's struck her colours," Ross shouted to Jeremy, who was on the small quarterdeck.

"Look at the broken yard. She's over to larboard. I doubt if she'll last much longer."

The *Vesta's* topsails were neatly reefed. Her jib, the only canvas she could carry in a storm, gave Ross some room for manoeuvre. Ross paused for a few seconds. He couldn't chance a shot, it would be too unpredictable in the heavy sea. Besides, the *Marie Claire's* incompetent crew were bringing about her demise themselves. But what of Bella? Convinced that she was there he had to stop and board the vessel, but he was already outrunning her.

"Get ready with the hooks," he shouted.

Jeremy looked at him aghast. "She'll take us with her."

"What would you have me do? Sail right past her?"

"No, but, surely we can stand off until the weather improves?"

"There's no time. She'll founder. If Bella's aboard, we might get ropes across and affect a rescue. They want Bella alive. Pray God that doesn't change."

"Aye aye, Captain. Starboard gun crew make ready with the hooks." Jeremy retreated to the lower deck to organize grappling irons.

* * * *

As the *Vesta's* dark shadow ran close by, Bella sighed. She was near but not near enough. Men threw out lines, but the distance between the two ships was too wide. The *Marie Claire* had no resistance left in her. Her angle of list increased. Her decks awash, she heaved once more, as if drawing her final breath before she capsized.

Bella clung to the ship's rigging as she was flung into the sea. The cold water stung her like a thousand needles being driven into her flesh. She shuddered and fought to keep her head above water. With waves washing over the *Marie Claire's* hull and her holds filling with water, Bella knew the ship was doomed. But her father's ship had run by. Friends were close, perhaps even Ross. She struggled to keep her arms and legs moving as the weight of her water-sodden velvet riding habit and the boat cloak pulled her down. She fought to keep her head on the surface and willed herself to stay with the floating wreckage for as long as possible. Crippled, the *Marie Claire* was on her side. Bella shivered. Somehow, she had to get out of the water. Her survival rested with her own determination to never give up.

In time, the *Vesta* would tack and return. She had to hold on. How many sea miles would the sloop run before the storm subsided? Rescue could be hours away. The sea would soon claim her if she didn't get out of the water. Frantically, she searched for something to aid her survival.

Dozens of empty barrels bobbed to the surface around her. She grabbed two and flung herself across them. Lying prostrate across the barrels, she prayed she could hold on until the *Vesta* returned.

* * * *

As the heavy storm clouds parted, Ross brought the *Vesta* about. He felt out of sorts, he hadn't eaten all day, and he had no appetite. The distress of losing the *Marie Claire* hung heavily upon him.

In the fading light, all hands searched the sea for survivors. They found a man in a thick coachman's coat, face down in the water. Jackson identified him as one of the Frenchies seen around Aston a few days previously. But he was dead when they fished him out of the sea.

As long as there remained a glimmer of hope that a person could survive in the water, Ross continued the search. He hated to lose, but acceptance of the inevitable began to gnaw at his innards. As each moment passed, he forced himself to face the possibility that the woman he loved was lost to him forever.

"Man in the water, off to starboard!" The call came from up top. All eyes turned in the same direction. A motionless body clad in a dark boat cloak lay stomach down over a barrel.

Ross ordered a boat to be lowered and lifted his glass to his eye. He took but a few seconds to focus on the pale face of the survivor. "The ship's yours, Jeremy. It's Bella."

Bella was unconscious when he reached her. Her hands were icy cold. He brushed salt from her face and gently touched her blue lips with his fingers. He felt her soft breath, and his heart swelled. "She's alive!"

Prizing her from the barrel, he pressed her closely to his chest, wrapped his arms around her, and willed some of his body heat into her. The men rowed them back to the *Vesta*. With most of the crew looking on, Ross carried the admiral's daughter to his cabin.

Inside, he laid her on the table. "Jackson, hot water and find some clothes. Ladies' clothing or anything suitable as long as they're clean and dry." The steward touched his cap. "And knock before you enter. I have to get Miss Richmond out of her wet garments."

"Aye aye, Captain."

Carefully Ross removed the boat cloak. It reminded him of the first time he had seen her in the derelict stable a few weeks ago. He cast the wet garment aside, realizing that it had probably saved her life. Next he cut the laces on her riding boots and gently removed them.

He searched for the fastenings on her riding habit. The buttons on the military style jacket were damp and proved too difficult for his fingers. He fumbled with the smallness of them. Bella's breathing became laboured. She needed to be dry and warm. He had to work faster. Tearing the bodice down the front, he eased her arms out of it. Her chemise and stays were also sodden through. Her body was extremely cold. Convinced that her pulse was weakening, he forced himself to hurry. There was no time for decorum. Bella's life might depend on his swift action.

Casting all sense of propriety aside, he stripped off her wet undergarments and placed a thick woollen blanket over her as he worked. She didn't move, and he grew more anxious for her welfare. Her lovely skin felt as cold as marble. He had to save her.

He rubbed her with the rough blanket, wrapped a cloth around her head to dry her hair, and picked her up in his arms. He felt an overwhelming desire to embrace her, as if holding her would prevent her slipping from this world. Desperate to warm her, he clasped her body to his. Silently he prayed that her life wasn't to be taken from him.

There was a knock on the door. He glanced over his shoulder. "Enter."

Jackson came in with a long white night shirt over his arm and a bucket of hot steaming water. "I found this, sir." He held up the garment. "Not a lady's apparel, but the best cotton."

"It will suffice." Ross nodded as he cradled Bella in his arms. "We must get her warm."

"I've asked the galley to heat some of the ballast stones. If they're wrapped in linen, they can be placed around her." Jackson placed the night shirt on the bed and set the bucket of water on the floor.

"Excellent idea, and make up some broth. Ask Mr. Thwaite to come here. Tell the men that Miss

Richmond remains unconscious, but we are making her as comfortable as we can."

Jackson left and Ross picked up the night shirt. He didn't want to let her go, but he had to get her dressed. Her head nestled on his shoulder, and he couldn't resist dropping soft, gentle kisses onto her forehead. Against his neck he felt the faint warmth of her breath. He gathered the nightshirt and placed it over her head. "Don't leave me, Bella. Please, not now when I've found my one true love." He pulled her arms through the sleeves as he continued to hold her, trying to warm her body with his.

There was a tap on the door. Jeremy stepped inside with concern etched on his face. "How is she?"

"No change. She's a little warmer, but still unconscious."

"Does she have any injuries; broken bones or signs of internal bleeding?"

Ross shook his head. "Only bruising around her wrists and ankles. Those villains must have had her tied up for some time. Her limbs appear sound, although she's dreadfully cold." He rubbed her body through the blanket as he spoke. "Pray that she's got the strength to hang on."

"She's young and strong. I'm sure she'll pull through."

Ross looked anxiously at his second-in-command. "Thank you. I pray so."

"Is there anything I can do?"

"Plot a course home, now that the storm has passed."

"Aye aye, Captain." He turned to leave but stopped before reaching the door. He glanced over his shoulder. "You asked me once where you could find a woman to match the *Diana's* dash, style, and courage. Do you remember?"

Ross looked up thoughtfully. "Yes, Jeremy, your first night at the Grange."

"You know you're holding her, don't you?"

Cradling Bella tightly to his chest, he answered, "Yes, Jeremy, I do."

* * * *

Admiral Richmond received news every day from Portsmouth. The message that his daughter might have been taken on board the *Marie Claire* hadn't surprised him, although he knew there was no proof. Hence, his men continued to search the port for further evidence.

He refused to contemplate his daughter's demise. However, the waiting was taking its toll on him. Stormy weather had been reported through the Western approaches. There had been no sightings of the *Vesta* or the *Marie Claire* by other ships. Each day he had been brought to the library by his manservants and spent most of his time with Lady Mary. They had discussed numerous scenarios and gone over the evidence several times.

"Do you really believe Granville is behind this diabolical plan?"

"I'm damn certain of it, Mary, but why? Have I wronged him? A marriage between them would have been disastrous, even if there had been the slightest compliance on her part. Their characters are incompatible. They would never have matched. Now Quentin, that's a different matter."

Lady Mary smiled as she plied her needle to her embroidery. After a few moments, she said, "Bella's in love with him. They would make a good match."

"Ah! You women and your good matches," he sighed. "What's a man to do?"

"In what manner?"

"In finding a wife, of course. First, a man must make his own way if he hasn't inherited money. Take my brother and myself. We were sent to the navy at the age of twelve. Arthur couldn't take to the life. He never got beyond mid-shipman, so he married a merchant's daughter in London and made his way in the tea trade."

"And Granville, was he their only child?"

"Yes."

"And his parents, what happened to them?"

"Both were taken with a fever during the hot spell back in ninety-seven. By that time, Granville had reached his majority. He took over the family affairs and within eighteen months had bankrupted himself. How he made his way after that, I do not know. He used to apply to me to settle his debts from time to time until I refused. I can think of no other reason for him to dislike me. But is that sufficient for him to do me harm?"

"Avarice can drive a man to extreme lengths."

"Yes, lass, it can. Granville is devious. He's not to be trusted, as well you know from his meddling tongue around the village. The audacity of the man, bragging that he was marrying my Bella."

"Perhaps he believed it? People can suffer from grand delusions, especially when they think themselves maligned by their kin."

"Maligned!" He coughed loudly. "When have I or Bella spoken ill of him? Privately, I admit, but never publically."

"After Bella, he is your heir."

"He is not! The estate's in trust for her, but should she—" He broke off, sealing his lips. His chin rested on his chest for several moments. When he lifted his head, he eyed her directly. "Granville will never inherit. It all goes to the naval hospital at Greenwich if I die without living issue."

"Very wise, Henry," she nodded, "very wise."

* * * *

Slowly Bella opened her eyes. Her lids were heavy as the cabin swam around her. A single lantern swung with the motion of the ship. Her head pounded. She closed her eyes and tried to piece together what had happened. Was she awakening from a dream or a terrifying nightmare?

She felt warm but remembered the cold, salty, and unrelenting waves of the sea. Now she was dry and lying on her back. Opening her eyes again, she realized she was inside. The room was bathed in moonlight, and the single yellow flame from the lantern danced over white painted panels. Content with her surroundings, she drifted back to sleep.

The next time she opened her eyes, dawn had replaced the silvery moonlight, and the lantern had burned out. Her mouth felt so dry she could hardly swallow. Her lips were rough and tasted of salt. Raising her head, she recognized the cabin of the *Vesta*. She let out a deep sigh and inwardly gave thanks to her Maker that somehow she had found her way aboard.

She turned her head towards the admiral's table and saw Ross hunched over it, asleep. His dark head rested on his folded arms and his long legs were stretched out. Overjoyed, she wanted to touch him and confirm that he was no illusion. He was only a few paces across the room. Taking a deep breath, she pushed herself up to a sitting position and swung her legs down from the bunk.

The deck felt cold under her bare feet. She fingered the oversized nightshirt and pushed the sleeves up her arms. Flexing her muscles, she stood upright. Finding her legs too weak to support her, she gripped the edge of the bed. It was but a short distance to the man she loved. Taking one small step, she inched forward.

The ship's bell sounded and Ross woke with a start. "Bella!"

With her arms outstretched she took another step towards him. In three swift strides, Ross crossed the cabin and caught her in his embrace. Safe in his arms, she felt his warm lips planting butterfly-like kisses across her forehead.

Hands raised, she touched his wavy hair and ran her fingers through the length of it. "I knew you'd come for me," she whispered, "as soon as I saw the *Vesta*. I knew it had to be you."

His firm hand caressed the nape of her neck and she took comfort in the strength of his body against hers. The powerful feeling of being held in his embrace once more was the finest medicine any physician could have prescribed. Drawing her closer he dropped a light kiss upon her dry lips. His mouth felt warm and moist against hers.

"I must have something to drink," she pleaded.

"And rest," he smiled. "I am so heartened that you've recovered consciousness. I will hear your story, but only when you have strength enough to tell it. Come, let me help you."

Willingly she placed herself in his care. Physically she felt drained of life, but emotionally her heart swelled with love. And when he swept her off her feet, elation and joy beyond measure welled up inside her. He returned her to the bunk and tucked the blanket around her. From across the cabin, she watched him fill a wine glass from the decanter and return to her side.

"Drink this," he said handing her the wine, "but not too quickly. Only sips at first. It will fortify you. I'll get Jackson to bring some broth." He drew up a stool and sat down.

The red wine tasted fruity, but she feared too much would send her to sleep and she wanted to talk to Ross. "The *Marie Claire*, I remember she capsized. I didn't see her go under, did she founder?"

"Yes, she was riding high in the water, short on cargo probably. By the time I could tack in the storm, she was under. She carried too much sail."

Bella took another sip of wine. "Were there any other survivors?"

Ross looked grim. "No. We hauled a man out of the sea, but he was dead. It took us some time to come about."

"A great compliment to your handling of this vessel in the storm." She gazed into his eyes.

He smiled back at her. "I have a good crew."

"What happened to my young groom, Watson?"

"Musket wound to the shoulder, but he was mending when we left."

"Thank goodness, I thought he had been killed when I saw him on the ground. Then someone grabbed me and—"

"There'll be ample time to go through all the details when we're home." He took her hand in his and squeezed it gently. "I was on my way to Witton that morning. After we parted in the long meadow, I felt I'd treated you badly. I had come to apologize for my abominable behaviour." He leaned towards her, rested his elbows on the bed, and drew her hand to his lips.

"It was my fault," she sighed. "I should never have sought you out like that, especially with your men looking on."

There was a knock at the door and Jackson entered. "Breakfast, Captain, Miss Richmond."

Chapter Fifteen

After breakfasting with Bella, Ross went up on deck. It was Jeremy's watch. "Bella says there are homing pigeons on board, any idea where they're kept?"

Jeremy looked blank. "Homing pigeons?"

"It appears that the admiral first heard of them in Naples and brought some back to Witton to breed. They are trained to fly home carrying short messages. He sends them to sea with his merchant ships. I'll take the rest of your watch. Ask Sanders if he knows where the pigeons are kept. We need to send a signal to the admiral."

"Aye aye, Captain."

Alone on the quarterdeck, Ross paced with his hands behind his back. At last he felt at ease. Bella was safe, and he was back at sea. He regretted the loss of the *Marie Claire*, but she had been taken by the storm, not by his doing. However, he was not prepared for the next truth which hit him keenly. Although he had hauled her out of the water, Bella had saved herself. Her quick thinking and dogged determination had prevailed. Getting herself to the floating barrels had saved her life, not he.

Ever watchful, he scanned the horizon, taking comfort in his own domain. Here, he had toiled through his teen years as a midshipman, passed his examination for lieutenant, and finally gained command. He had served with many men, all good sailors, but only a handful would have acted with Bella's tenacity when faced with ferocious sea conditions. How he admired her. How he loved her. How much he wanted to marry her.

An overwhelming surge of guilt threatened to drown his previous good humour. He gripped the ship's rail until his knuckles were white. Would a union between them condemn her to a life of loneliness the moment he left English shores? Was he acting selfishly?

He drew his consolation from the sea and scanned the horizon again. The *Vesta* was alone, but he was in familiar waters. What English sailor didn't enjoy the run home? With her canvas unfurled and the Westerlies filling her sails, the *Vesta* would make Portsmouth by tomorrow afternoon. Sooner, if the wind didn't drop.

Jeremy returned with a wicker cage containing two fat pigeons. "I rescued these from the galley. They're the only two left."

"Send this signal, same for each, 'B safe home Friday, Q.'"

"Aye aye, Captain."

"And, Jeremy, get some sleep."

Although neither wore a uniform, the lieutenant saluted, and the captain returned the compliment.

Alone again, Ross's thoughts returned to Bella. It surprised him how distracting females could be. Perhaps it was the reason he had long resisted wives on board ship. Or was it his mother's abandonment of him as a boy? He forced himself to think deeply on the matter. He concluded that the answer was a mixture of the two. However, the more he thought of Bella, the more he asked himself a simple question. Did he want to be parted from her again?

Since Bella had been snatched from him and placed in mortal danger, he realised how important she was to him. Tonight would probably be their last night together at sea. He decided to open his heart to her and renew his proposal. But could he give up the sea?

That question was the hardest of all to answer truthfully. He was thirty-two years old. He had been at sea for twenty years. One day he would have to give up the life, but was he ready to retire now? The past few days confirmed one overriding fact of his life—the sea ran through his veins.

Bonaparte dominated the Continent, his greed for power and territory insatiable. Would he set his sights on England and break the Peace Treaty? In his heart, Ross wanted to marry Bella, but he could not promise her, in all honesty, that he would never go to sea again.

*** *

Admiral Richmond sat in the library reading the *Naval Chronicle*. He tossed it aside when Middleton entered.

"There's a message, sir, from one of the *Vesta's* homing pigeons."

"Quickly, fetch Lady Mary. She's in the flower garden." When Middleton stepped outside, the admiral said a short prayer for his daughter's safe return. He had forced all thoughts of her demise from his mind because he knew it would break his heart if he lost her.

Lady Mary rushed inside from the garden, carrying a selection of cut flowers in her basket and followed by Middleton. "What news, Henry? Are you comfortable there?" Abandoning her basket, she bent down to adjust the cushion supporting his injured leg.

"Yes, yes. Don't fuss. I'm bracing myself," he said. "The news must be urgent to have come by carrier pigeon. And if it were the worst, Quentin would have come in person, wouldn't he?"

Lady Mary nodded. "Yes, I believe he would have. Charles always tried to visit the next of kin when he lost one of his people."

The admiral turned to his butler. "Open the file, Middleton. I'm too nervous to trust the task to my own hand."

The butler did as he was bid. "It reads: B safe home Friday, Q."

"Bye Jove, excellent news. What a relief? Eh, Mary?"

She jumped to her feet and clapped her hands. "I'm delighted. Oh, Henry, I'm so happy. I knew Captain Quentin wouldn't let us down."

The admiral thought for a few moments. "Middleton, you have my permission to share the good news with the rest of the staff. Tell them Miss Richmond is safe and we expect her back from her sea voyage on Friday. That will be all."

"Yes, sir."

As soon as the door closed behind the butler, the admiral turned to Lady Mary. "When is he going to ask her?"

"If you refer to marriage, then I believe he did propose and was rejected."

"What?" he roared. "Nobody tells me anything around here. When? What do you mean rejected? Did Bella send him away?"

"As far as I'm aware, she did."

"Why? What's wrong with the fellow? Wasn't half the county after him?"

"That was the general belief, and as you know Quentin's arrival in the neighbourhood did cause something of a stir. And I remember Bella teasing him over it. As for her part, I think she got a little confused."

"Confused, how? Talk to me plainly. What went wrong?"

"Well, Henry, initially she refused because she didn't wish to be married to anyone. Or at least she thought so."

"Why not? Don't all women want to be married?"

"Bella could see no advantage for herself. She had the management of this establishment and you to look after. Why did she need a husband?"

"God's teeth, Mary! Isn't the reason bloody obvious?"

Lady Mary coughed. "Henry, we're not on board ship—"

"Sorry, my dear, I forgot myself. But you were never one to stand on ceremony. All those years on board with Rufford I'll wager there's not much that you haven't heard."

She raised her eyebrows. "That's as may be, but there are some topics which don't go beyond the gangplank, as well you know."

"Understood, lass." He nodded. "Please continue."

"When you were injured, she felt obliged to remain and look after you."

"Bah! I'll never understand the workings of a female mind."

"Of course, you didn't help by talking about Colonel Quentin and his new offspring. Didn't you hint that perhaps you might remarry yourself?"

"Oh, I said it to get her thinking that Quentin was the man for her. He'd already asked me if he could approach her. Damn good fellow. Why the hell can't she see it and say yes to him?"

"Are we at sea again, Henry?"

"But, Mary, this is you and me talking. You understand these things. You know the language and don't take offence."

"Fortunate for you that I don't, isn't it? Now, why do you think Bella turned him down?"

"I don't bloody know," he said, raising his voice. "Tell me!"

"She doesn't think she could stand the long separation when he's at sea."

Henry Richmond remained silent. Over the years, he had heard of numerous marriages strained by separation and known officers who described themselves as strangers to their wives when they were set ashore. He had suffered anguish himself, especially during the first week out. As the weeks turned into months, the responsibility of duty usually took over. Home became a dream where only the finer moments were recalled, not the discontent and awkwardness. "Is that why Rufford insisted on taking you with him?"

She nodded. "Our circumstances were unusual. I had no family to return to until my father died and my brother inherited. And we were not blessed. The decision may have been different with children."

They sat in silence for a few moments until the admiral, looking at her with fresh eyes, said, "I can easily solve Bella's misguided problem of paternal obligation, but I cannot resolve her aversion to an absent husband."

"I'm sure that with Bella's tenacious spirit and Quentin's natural ability for leadership, they will soon find that their future lies in the same direction."

"And what of you, Mary? Where does your future lie?"

"Me?" she grinned. "I'm destined to be a favourite aunt, chief family correspondent, and permanent chaperone to Miss 'Never to Marry' Richmond." She laughed.

"How about adding another label to your considerable repertoire?"

"And what would that be?"

"Marry me, Mary."

She didn't answer.

His heart felt heavy. Had he pushed her too far? "I can't promise you the first flush of love," he said, "but I think you're a damn fine woman and, by God, a wonderful companion. I know I've been unbearable since I broke my leg, but each day has been made better by your presence. How about it, lass? Let's shock the county, nay the country, by putting up the banns."

"And I was beginning to think you would never ask, Henry."

* * * *

Ross entered the cabin and smiled at Bella. What a delightful picture she made. The sea water had curled her fair hair. She had tied it back, but a few stray tendrils had escaped the ribbon meant to hold them and twisted attractively around her face.

It pleased him to see her cheeks had regained their colour, which was more than could be said for her riding habit. The sea water had taken much of the dark blue, leaving behind a varied hue of pale green patches. Her jacket must have shrunk, for it was open at the front, exposing a white bodice. On closer examination, he noticed that most of the small brass buttons were missing.

Jackson entered the cabin and laid the table. Glancing at the number of places, Ross wondered who'd been invited. A wave of disappointment flowed over him. He had hoped to be alone with her.

"I've asked Mr. Thwaite, Mr. Sanders, and Lieutenant Collins to join us. I want to express my gratitude to the whole ship's company for saving my life, but I can't have everyone to dinner, can I?"

"You could give them all an extra ration of your father's rum." Ross suggested and, turning to Jackson, asked, "Is there sufficient?"

"Yes, sir. Not much meat," he said, "but there's plenty of grog."

"With your permission, Miss Richmond?" Ross looked directly at Bella, who nodded her approval. Turning to Jackson, he said, "Give the men an extra ration tonight. And explain that it's with Miss Richmond's compliments."

"Aye aye, Captain."

* * * *

When the guests trooped in, Bella noticed their behaviour was remarkably reserved, except for Mr. Thwaite, whose amiable character shone through his broad smile. Lieutenant Collins wore his best uniform; the others only had the clothes they stood up in, having boarded in haste.

The poached fish was tender, the accompanying vegetables bland, and the puddings, two differing varieties, in need of sugar. Jackson apologized profusely. Bella sat at the head of the table with Ross on her right and Mr. Thwaite on her left. The other two guests were next to them. The men kept their conversation polite, which was probably due to her presence. But their polished manners didn't fool her for one moment. Mildly amused, she doubted that her father had ever hosted such a subdued meal while on board. The dinners he held at Witton for his gentlemen were much noisier.

"I must be about my business," Mr. Sanders said, rising to his feet. "I thank you, Miss Richmond, for your warm hospitality. Everyone is delighted and relieved that you have recovered from your ordeal."

"Thank you," she replied.

"If you will also excuse me?" Lieutenant Collins said.

"Certainly, Lieutenant," Bella said. "I hope my father and I will have the pleasure of your company again, either here or at Witton."

"Thank you Miss Richmond. Please carry my good wishes to the admiral for his speedy recovery." The lieutenant bowed and left.

When he had gone, Mr. Thwaite said, "Has Ross told you that he's promised to be my groomsman at my forthcoming nuptials?"

"I believe your sister remarked upon it at the ball. Has the date been finalized?"

"At long last we're signed, sealed, and delivered. With the amount of time it has taken to draw up a settlement, I believe we would have done better making a run for Gretna."

"Wouldn't that have brought the mighty Glen clan chasing after you?" Ross asked.

Mr. Thwaite nodded. "Probably, but Gretna would have suited me. I would have preferred a speedy ceremony and no interference from my prospective in-laws. However, we must pay our dues to fashion and stand up at St. George's in Hanover Square."

"And does Miss Glen share your view?" Bella asked.

"I'm pleased to say she does. We are both eagerly anticipating the day. She tells me she would marry me tomorrow if I provided the transportation and the preacher. However, her mother is determined to keep her other daughters in town. They cannot afford to miss the Season. Elizabeth has several sisters, each of whom is expected to marry well. Why, once they knew Ross was ashore, they wouldn't leave him alone in London. They hounded him at the theatre and attended the same balls. No wonder he chose to bury himself in the country."

"That's not true," Ross said. "You know how town bores me. Once my business with the Admiralty and my agent was done, I was anxious to see the estate I'd rented."

"So that was your excuse?" Mr. Thwaite leaned towards Bella and added, "Let me tell you one of his secrets, Miss Richmond. Ross has spent the last six years pursuing every vessel flying French colours that he could find, and the minute he steps onto English soil he becomes the quarry. How ironic! The hunter becomes the hunted. In the end, Miss Richmond, he had to seek refuge in the countryside."

"Oh, now I understand, Captain, the reason for the frequency of your calls. Any port in a storm?" She teased.

"Nothing of the sort," Ross said, his eyes gleaming at her as he spoke.

"I have to check on deck," Mr. Thwaite said, getting to his feet. "Ships have an unusual habit of finding trouble during a young middy's watch."

Bella noticed how Ross raised a disbelieving eyebrow at his friend's excuse to quit the cabin. When Mr. Thwaite had gone, he poured her another glass of red wine and handed it to her. As she took it from him, she thought he looked troubled. "What's the matter?"

"I think there's something you should know about Mr. Granville Richmond."

She took a swift breath. She had hoped to hear no more of her cousin.

"You know he wanted to inherit your father's estate?"

"Yes," she sighed. "He has been a disappointment to our family for many years. For as long as I can remember the problem has always been financial. As to the estate, he has made no secret of the fact that he regarded himself as my father's heir. When he had the audacity to propose to me, he claimed that marriage was a way of keeping father's money in the family!"

"Was that ever the admiral's wish?"

"Of course not! Papa disliked him from childhood." She took a sip of wine, feeling the need of fortification if she had to talk at length about her cousin. "Do you suspect he was involved in my kidnapping?"

"Yes, and behind the attempt on your father's life."

"Oh dear! While I have been resting here in the cabin, I couldn't help reviewing everything that has happened. Only one name came to mind."

"Your cousin?"

She nodded. "What drives a man to contrive such a vile plan involving his own kin? Captain Artois said he'd been paid to take me to France, where I was to be married, but he didn't name his employer. I cannot prove it was my cousin. I dare say he intended to finish Father off too and inherit everything himself. Naturally I was relieved when I realized they needed me alive. Although I doubt I would have survived long in France once we'd been through a bogus ceremony."

"I'm afraid there is more."

She looked up at him sharply. She could see from his expression that he had bad news. Inwardly she prepared herself. "My father?"

"No, I am pleased to report he was master-minding the search for you from his armchair the last time I saw him. He gave me written permission to take the *Vesta* to sea. I speak once more of Mr. Granville Richmond. He won the Grange from Sir Humphrey in a card game."

Bella gasped. "But how?"

"He probably cheated, but again, there is no proof and it is said that Sir Humphrey took his own life."

"Oh my goodness! How dreadful for his family. But what will you do?"

"I hold the lease until next Lady Day. He can't evict me until then." He smiled at her. "I'm sure I might find some kind person prepared to board me when I have to quit the place. But more importantly, how will you take to your cousin as a neighbour?"

"He hates the country, so he'll not stay there long. Then there'll be the inevitable string of tenants. If only we could prove his involvement in my kidnap."

"I have an agent investigating his affairs in London. Until we have evidence, Richmond cannot be charged with any crime. But I'm convinced that justice will be done one day."

"I hope so," she said softly.

Bella leaned towards him, her fingers nearly touching his. "You said that you were coming to Witton to speak to me on the day of the kidnap. What were you going to say?"

He edged nearer to her, covered her hand with his, and with his shoulder almost touching hers, said, "I wanted to apologize. The way I treated you was abominable. I sent you packing without a word of kindness or consideration. I'm ashamed. My behaviour was dishonourable. I felt embarrassed because my men were watching, but their presence should not have been my excuse. Can you forgive me?"

"Of course I can, and when I compare my behaviour to yours, it is I who should ask your forgiveness. I acted impetuously when I came to the meadow. I had no right to disturb you while you were working on the land. When I thought I'd received your note, my heart ruled my head. I'm afraid I rushed out of the house without a second thought."

"And fortunately, you left my 'so-called' note behind."

"So that's how you knew where to start looking for me! I wondered what had first set you off, for I knew there was no talk of ransom. When I found myself on board a ship, I thought I was being transported to Africa into slavery. It was only when I spoke to Captain Artois that I realized he was delivering me to France."

Ross brushed a stray tendril of hair away from her face.

Aware of his closeness, she felt his hand gently squeeze hers. "Can you imagine how elated I felt when I spied the *Vesta* coming up behind us? It couldn't have been Papa. It had to be you."

"You were on deck in the storm?"

"I managed to escape from the captain's cabin. The ship was under-crewed. They couldn't spare a hand to guard me. Once on deck, I could see the sails poorly reefed. The mainsail had broken loose, taking the yard with it."

"At least her captain had the sense to haul down her colours. Otherwise I might have been accused of attempting to fire on a friendly ship."

Bella's mouth dropped open. "You planned to attack her!"

"Initially, but when I saw what a chaotic state she was in, it wasn't necessary. I doubt if I could have gotten a decent shot at her. The sea was running against us. We tried to get lines across, but the storm took us past."

"Oh, Ross, you risked a court martial for me?"

"I thought only of you. We scoured Portsmouth for information until we heard someone fitting your description had been taken aboard the *Marie Claire*. But we were too late, she sailed on the evening tide. My plan was simple—to stop and search her, even if I had to run up the skull and cross bones to do so."

"You'd have resorted to piracy to save me?"

"Yes, Bella, I would."

"Then I am very glad, Ross, that the storm saved you from dishonour," she whispered and kept silent about her part in striking the French tri-colours.

"But it claimed yet another ship for Davy Jones's locker."

"Did it? I blame the *Marie Claire's* captain and crew for her loss. What calibre of merchantman puts to sea without cargo or ballast? She was running too high in the water, and when we capsized, she bobbed around like a cork. All those empty barrels, I thanked God for them, as they must have kept the ship afloat for some time. What I can't understand is why there weren't more survivors."

"That we'll never know," he murmured. He was sitting so close to her that she could feel his warm breath on her face. "You, my love, were saved and that is all that matters to me. I love you, Bella. There is no other woman in the world for me. And no other woman I could love more. Marry me, Bella, marry me. I'll willingly live at Witton Abbey if that's what you want, as long as I can be with you."

Bella gazed into his clear blue eyes. Her heart raced. "I love you, Ross Quentin," she said without reserve or shame. "I think I've loved you from the moment I first saw you when you rescued me. There's nothing I want more than to be your wife. But what of your concerns about our being apart when you return to your command?"

"Oh, my love," he sighed as he dropped a gentle kiss on her forehead and gazed into her eyes. "I was wrong about taking wives to sea. You're so very different from all the officer's wives I've encountered in my career. In truth, Bella Richmond, I would go to sea with you any day."

"And I with you, my love."

Epilogue

Double weddings were not uncommon in the parish of Aston, but those involving gentry were most unusual. One month after rescuing Bella from the sea, Ross stood outside the church, waiting for his bride. He wore his best dress uniform, his post captain's epaulettes glistening in the morning sunshine. "What time is it?"

Jeremy, standing as groomsman, flicked open his gold pocket watch. "About two minutes later than when you last asked. Don't say you're getting nervous."

"I hate the waiting. I used to get the same feeling on the day of a battle in a man-of-war, waiting for the admiral's signal. It was why I always wanted to command a frigate, never a ship of the line."

"They'll be here soon. It's a tradition. Brides always come late to their weddings."

Ross's eagle eyes spotted a dark carriage heading towards the village. It turned into the high street and halted outside the lych-gate. It bore a crest. "It's the Lord Norton's carriage. He'll have Lady Mary with him. We must try to stop them descending."

They rushed to the carriage and greeted the occupants. "The Richmonds haven't arrived yet," Jeremy said.

"I can't think what's keeping them," Ross added.

✳ ✳ ✳ ✳

"You look lovely, my dear," the admiral said to his daughter as she descended the stairs. "I could not bear to give you away to a lesser man than Quentin. A man could have no better son-in-law."

"And I cannot imagine a finer stepmother than Lady Mary. But, Papa, we must make haste. We do not want to be late for our own weddings, do we?"

Middleton opened the double front doors of Witton Abbey and two manservants brought the admiral his crutches. "I can manage," he protested.

"Please, Papa, let them help you. You want to be strong enough to stand up in church."

"Yes," he panted, his face locked into a tight grimace. "We must get to the church."

The sound of a carriage stopping in the drive drew Bella's attention away from her father. "Middleton, who is that?"

"The carriage bears no crest, Miss, but the gentleman descending is Mr. Richmond."

"Granville Richmond!" Bella felt her stomach clench and a cold shiver made her shudder.

The admiral pulled himself up on his crutches as his unwelcome visitor stepped into the hall. "What do you want?"

Removing his hat, Richmond made a flamboyant bow. "Greetings Uncle Richmond, cousin Arabella, I have come personally to extend my most joyous congratulations on your forthcoming nuptials."

"How dare you present yourself on my threshold this day, or any day!"

Richmond turned his head slightly; his large cravat and stiff pointed collar restricted his movement. "As the new owner of Aston Grange and your nearest kin, I thought it only civil to show my respects."

"Respects? I want none from you. I warned you once never to darken my threshold again. Haven't you caused enough trouble to Bella and me?"

"Trouble, sir? I have no notion of your meaning. What am I accused of? I agree there was a slight misunderstanding between Miss Richmond and myself, but that is all forgotten, especially today when she is to marry Quentin."

"You, sir, are guilty of cheating Sir Humphrey out of his estate!"

Richmond tilted his nose in the air. "I won Aston Grange fair and square."

"Yes, that's what you say. I say you drove the man to suicide. And what of your involvement with the abductions?"

"Abductions?" Richmond looked puzzled. "Who has been abducted?"

Bella nearly cried out. She wanted to rail against her cousin for appearing unannounced and unwelcome on their doorstep, especially on today of all days. But there were servants present, and she feared her father might reveal more about their affairs than seemed prudent. "Young women have been kidnapped throughout this part of south Hampshire. It is said French privateers are responsible."

"You astound me, cousin, I have heard nothing of these matters."

"That I do not believe," the admiral said. "You are up to your neck in this foul business."

"Goodness, sir!" Richmond looked affronted. "If you were not my uncle, I'd call you out!"

"Ha! Call me out indeed! I am your uncle and I am turning you off my land. Whether you own Aston Grange or not, from this day, I disown you. Do you understand? I do not wish to cast eyes on you again. Middleton, see Mr. Richmond to his carriage."

Bella watched her cousin's nostrils flare and his face redden. She thought he was about to speak, but instead he turned quickly and strode out of the door. She rushed to her father and grasped his arm. "Oh, Papa, I thought we had seen the last of him."

"So had I, my dear, but something tells me our dealings with Mr. Granville Richmond are not at an end. He has much to answer for when evidence can be found to incriminate him. And, my dear, he is our kin. The responsibility is mine, and mine alone. I shall not rest until I have brought him to justice."

* * * *

Not wishing to enter the church until her bridegroom arrived, Lady Mary had retreated to the parsonage, accompanied by her brother and his wife.

"You are most welcome at our humble establishment." Mrs. Winters curtseyed several times to the Earl and Countess of Norton.

"Thank you for your kindness," Lady Mary said, a little concerned that the admiral and Bella were late. It was so unlike Henry.

When they were seated in the best parlour, Mrs. Winters said, "I don't know what has happened to the neighbourhood of late. The admiral's sheep slaughtered for no apparent reason, then his hunting accident. And there are dreadful tales about young women being abducted from their homes in the county. Fortunately none of our parishioners have gone missing, but whatever next? I live in fear of what may happen."

Lady Mary glanced at her brother and sister-in-law and willed them to keep silent. The truth about Bella's abduction was not generally known since the crew of the *Vesta* had been sworn to silence and the main perpetrators had gone down with the *Marie Claire*. Any suggestion that Bella had fallen into the hands of brigands could only injure her reputation and that of her family. "I'm sure peace will soon return to our community, Mrs. Winters."

"I blame the Peace Treaty, Lady Mary. Without the peace there wouldn't have been seamen and privateers roaming the countryside with nothing to do but cause trouble. They should be at sea, fighting for King and country. Protecting us."

"An admirable sentiment," Lord Norton agreed, "but many families would have been denied the pleasure of seeing their nearest and dearest."

"And there has been a wave of matches this Season due to the many officers finding themselves on shore," Lady Norton added.

"Of course—what was that?" Mrs. Winters jumped to her feet. "I believe I hear a carriage approaching." She flung open the window. "The admiral and Miss Richmond are here!"

"At last," Lady Mary sighed. "I can think of nothing better than to proceed to the church to get married."

* * * *

As Bella left the church in her husband's carriage, she felt the happiest of brides. Despite the turmoil of meeting her cousin, she refused to allow him to come between her and Ross. She looked into her bridegroom's eyes. "I am so proud to be a captain's wife."

"And I am the proudest of men to have married the admiral's daughter." He kissed her cheek. "I love you, Bella Quentin."

About the Author

Lynda Dunwell is a LSE graduate and has taught economics and business studies for twenty years. She has worked as a press officer, advertisement copy writer and tourist information officer.

She read Jane Austen and Georgette Heyer novels in her teens and still continues. She is a member of the UK Romantic Novelists' Association and adores Regency life, including clothes, games, houses, pastimes and even food!

Lynda is a keen student of genealogy and has traced her paternal family line back to 1485. Currently she is researching her female line which she describes as "far more challenging."

Although based in the landlocked English Midlands, Lynda loves the sea and adores cruising. She finds Regency history fascinating especially King George III's navy because there was a captaincy in every midshipman's tool bag.

Website: http://www.lyndadunwell.com

If you have enjoyed Marrying the Admiral's Daughter then why not read the sequel, Captain Westwood's Inheritance?

Available from Amazon in print and ebook format

41092870R00156

Made in the USA
Charleston, SC
20 April 2015